Love on the Bayfront

Ginger Woods Brodess

I love my southern roots and the influence it's had on my life. To the great southern people who've inhabited my heart....love you bunches.

To my readers who felt this story wasn't finished. I love the characters of this book and getting to explore their lives a little further. Thanks for pushing me for another book.

To my editor (and niece) Taylor Worden, thank you for pushing me to be a better writer and for making this book a better finished product. You have a bright future! Love you.

To my husband Doug, for supporting me through all my creative, sometimes frustrating, endeavours. Much love.

Contents

INTRODUCTION

"I remember every time I've made you blush, how you looked when you were soaked from head to toe from the waterfall, and the night when I held you close for the very first time," Sebastian knelt down in front of Isabel. "The night we rode through the park in the carriage and you placed your hand on my thigh nearly drove me crazy. Every single moment I've spent with you has never been forgotten," he chuckled in spite of himself, "and believe me, I've tried."

Sebastian pulled Isabel to her feet and held on tightly to her hands. "And while I've been on the receiving end of your feisty side, trust me on that, I've also been on the receiving end of your loving side," he softened as he looked in Izzy's eyes. "I've fought this for so long, not knowing if I was the right guy for you. And I still don't know that for sure Isabel Porter, but I know without a shadow of a doubt that you're the right girl for me."

Tears streamed down Izzy's face as Sebastian finished his dialogue. She couldn't seem to find the words to respond.

"I love you," whispered Sebastian. He stopped long enough to see what his latest revelation would reveal from Izzy.

"Well?" asked Sebastian impatiently.

"I was just wondering what took you so long," answered Izzy, crying and laughing at the same time. She threw her arms around Sebastian in disbelief and delight.

When Sebastian finally pulled away, he lifted Izzy's chin and kissed her with the same passion he had felt for so long. Izzy melted into his touch and prayed the moment would never end.

Chapter 1

The night of Sebastian's confession had played itself out in Isabel's mind over and over again this past year. Izzy could still feel the warmth of his arms and hear the ring in his voice as he declared his love for her in Ms. Dottie's backyard. Those sweet memories only haunted her now. The pain from their split was still so deep it often felt like it had just happened.

Isabel sat on the bench beside the big oak tree facing the bay. Even though she had only arrived in Fairhope a few months back, Izzy had already claimed this little spot of heaven, spending most afternoons enjoying the sun setting over the bay before she retreated to her apartment for the evening.

When Ms. Dottie had called a few months back and asked if she would come back to Alabama and run the family bookstore, Izzy wasn't sure what to think about this new request. She had loved living in Mobile with Ms. Dottie when she was sent there to freelance by her magazine. During that year, Ms. Dottie had become family. When Dottie's sister suddenly became ill and passed away, she called Izzy to see if she could come for a while and help run the family store in Fairhope.

It had been years since Dottie had visited the bookstore. She had never been involved in the family business. Now that she was the only family member left, she had to decide what to do with the store that had been handed down through her family for generations. She was too old to maintain it by herself, and that's when Isabel Porter's name came to mind. After all, she was like family now.

Dottie didn't know how Izzy would respond after her break up with Sebastian Hadley. She knew enough about her pretty young friend and the charming young man that coming back to Alabama might be the last thing she would be willing to do. But Dottie figured it was worth a try until she could figure things out, so she gave Izzy a call.

Isabel sat silent, staring out at the bay, fighting back memories that only the state of Alabama could bring. When she left a year ago, her heart was soaring on wings of love. Sebastian Hadley had gently weaved his way into her life during the year she had spent in Mobile. It wasn't an instantaneous attraction but a slow and gradual one. They had a friendship that slowly blossomed into something more.

When Izzy left to go back home, she had full confidence they could make their long-distance relationship work. Bash came to the city to visit her a few times and she traveled back to Alabama. But there were still uncertainties she struggled with while they were apart. Insecurity and jealousy drove her feelings about Sebastian's group of friends, especially the girls. They began to argue and nit-pick with one another until Sebastian finally decided it just wasn't fun anymore and said they should go their separate ways. And that was that.

"I guess love really doesn't overcome all," Isabel mumbled to herself as she picked up her things and headed towards her apartment that was just above the bookstore.

Ms. Dottie knew there was a make-shift apartment upstairs when she asked Izzy to come back and help. She realized with a little bit of money and handy men working around the clock, the once bare apartment would provide a cozy little place that Isabel could call home.

Every time Izzy entered the apartment, she couldn't believe how well the décor suited her style. As Ms. Dottie explained, "I added a little bit of you with a little bit of me." Izzy walked over to the small white table that sat in the corner to drop off her purse. She loved having a small writing desk that overlooked main street below. She found it quite entertaining watching people when they thought no one was looking.

Izzy made her way over to the couch that sat across the room. Kicking off her shoes, she curled her legs up under her and pulled out a blanket from inside the old vintage trunk that sat in front of the couch. Even though it had only been a short time since Izzy's arrival in Fairhope, this little apartment was already a welcome sight after a long day in the store. She curled up on the couch, closed her eyes and drifted off to sleep thinking about sweet Ms. Dottie and how well she knew what brought her comfort.

Chapter 2

Isabel was reminded of how humid mornings are in the south, as she strolled to get her morning cup of coffee, feeling as if the air was sticking to her skin.

Camille's Café had been a must since she arrived. Izzy stumbled into the café the first morning she was in town and had made it her first stop every day since.

"Morning Camille," Isabel said as she dragged herself into the warm and cozy spot.

"Mornin' Iz," answered Camille, "do you want the usual?"

"I'm so tired," groaned Isabel, "maybe you can just hook me up to an IV so the coffee drips through my veins all day."

Camille laughed at her new-found friend. Izzy arrived every morning with a droopy look on her face and by the time she left had a new kick in her step.

"I see that Tristan James has been spending a lot of time at your store these days," Camille winked as she handed Isabel her coffee.

"Now Camille, don't be going around spreading small town rumors. Tristan has been helping me get things fixed at the bookstore. That's all."

"Whatever you say Ms. Izzy," laughed Camille. "Whatever you say."

Isabel smiled, shaking her head as she looked out the window, sipping her warm cup of coffee. This quaint little town had felt like home right away. As she watched store owners begin to open their shops down Main Street, Isabel recognized her cue that it was time to get herself in gear and head to the bookstore.

To say that Ms. Dottie hadn't fully explained the condition of the bookstore would be an understatement. In her defense, she had no idea what the store looked like either. Her sister had been sick for quite a while, and in the meantime, Bayfront Books had been left unattended. Everything was dusty, outdated and needed a good scrubbing along with a fresh coat of paint. That's how Isabel had met Tristan James. He ran the hardware store down the street. She had made many trips to the store for supplies until Tristan eventually started making special deliveries to the store. His southern, gentlemanly ways were shining through and she didn't mind the help at all. As she neared the store, she noticed Tristan was waiting for her to get there and open up.

"Well, look what the dog drug in," teased Tristan.

"Not all of us get up at the break of dawn to go to work," replied Izzy with a grin.

Tristan carried the paint inside after Izzy unlocked the door. Although the store had been passed down in the family for generations, the way Isabel found it suggested no one had given it any tender loving care for a very long time.

Books were piled up on tops of shelves and packed in boxes in every corner, while displays hung empty. The chipped paint signaled a need for a fresh new look. Isabel and Dottie spent hours working to perk the place up, setting several of Dottie's old heirlooms in the store window to give the store a touch of family tradition.

She began to show Tristan the places in the store that needed touched up as well, needing a handy man who could patch holes and make some repairs. Izzy climbed up a ladder that was standing near a tall bookcase, inspecting the cracked walls. Pointing out water damage on the wall, her foot suddenly missed a rung and slipped. Tristan grabbed her by the waist and steadily guided her to the floor. Isabel smiled in thanks, turning her head as she heard the bell on the front door began to jingle. She looked up to see Bash and Asher carrying in an antique roll top desk. Sebastian's eyes widened as he saw Isabel for the first time in a year. It also didn't take long for him to assess the scene of Tristan's hands wrapped around her waist. The tension in the room could be cut with a knife.

"Sorry to interrupt," Sebastian stammered, "but Ms. Dottie called and asked if I would bring a few items of hers over to the family bookstore in Fairhope." His brows lifted in surprise while he couldn't shake the grimace covering his face.

"Hey Iz," exclaimed Asher, walking over to give her a hug. "I didn't realize you were back in the area."

"That makes two of us," mumbled Sebastian, trying to compose himself.

"Uh, yeah," Isabel replied quickly stepping out of Tristan's grasp and moving towards the nearest bookcase to straighten up a pile of books. "Ms. Dottie called and asked if I could help with the bookstore she'd just inherited from her family. Her sister ran it for years but passed away recently. Ms. Dottie had no one else she trusted, so she called me to see if I could help out for a while."

Sebastian didn't look like he was interested in small talk, so she quickly showed him and Asher where to put the roll top desk; next to one of the front windows. As the guys made their way back out to the truck to retrieve the next item, Tristan excused himself, stating he needed to get back to work and leaving Isabel to deal with the awkwardness he just observed.

"Where do you want this one?" asked Sebastian with a chill in his voice.

"Just set it up in the other window and I'll rearrange it later,"

Isabel said, continuing to flutter about the store trying to keep herself busy.

Sebastian set the table down with a thud and walked back outside. Asher stood there not knowing what to do or say. He moved closer to Izzy so he wouldn't have to shout across the store.

"So, I'm guessing that Bash didn't know you were back in town," asked Asher with hesitancy in his voice.

Isabel never looked up when she replied, "you would be guessing right."

The door jingled again and there stood Sebastian, hands on his hips and cheek twitching in anger. Asher quickly made up an excuse and was out the door before either of the estranged love birds could utter a word.

"Did you ever plan on telling me that you were back in the area?" demanded Sebastian.

"I really haven't taken time to think about it…" replied Izzy before being interrupted by Sebastian's outburst.

"Time? You couldn't take two minutes to make a call or send a text?" Sebastian was pacing and she knew he was furious.

"And what exactly did you want me to say?" Isabel fired back. "The girl you said you loved, then walked out on, is living across the bridge from you now."

"I don't recall it going down quite like that. In fact, I'd say it was rather mutual," shouted Sebastian.

"Would you please stop yelling at me?" Isabel fired back.

He turned to look out the store window. He deliberately began to take deep breaths to calm himself down. He roamed around the store, picking up books but not really looking at them, and finally turned to face Izzy.

"I'm sorry I was yelling at you. It just took me by surprise when I opened the door and there you stood. With another guy's hands wrapped around your waist, by the way. You were the last person I was expecting to see."

"And I'm truly sorry about that. I should have already called. I just didn't know what to say," sighed Izzy. "I didn't know if I was ready to see you again. Heck, I didn't know if you would ever want to see *me* again."

"Well, being in another guy's arms wouldn't have been my first choice," responded Sebastian, slightly chuckling.

Isabel started telling him the whole story about Ms. Dottie calling and wanting to know if she would run the store for her. Talking ninety miles a minute, Isabel didn't even notice how quiet Sebastian had become. She turned to see what he was doing and found him sitting on a stool listening to her very intently.

"What are you doing?"

"I was just sitting here thinking about how much I've missed your babbling," laughed Sebastian. "And just how much I've missed that laugh."

Izzy locked eyes with Bash from across the room. Her heart sank to her feet as butterflies did somersaults in the pit of her stomach.

"So, what's the deal with perfect Ken doll?" asked Sebastian trying not to show how much that scene was annoying to him.

"There's nothing going on with Tristan. That's his name for the record. He works at the hardware store down the street and I've been there so many times picking up supplies that we've become friends."

"Friends?" asked Sebastian. "Like we were friends?"

"That subjects off the table," replied Izzy and continued to tell him about the bookstore and how much work needed to be done just to make it look presentable.

Bash walked around the store to assess the damage. Books were stacked everywhere as if nothing had been organized in quite some time and a thick blanket of dust covered the shelves. It had an aroma of musty old books and mold. Several places in the room had holes that needed to be patched up and painted. Bash climbed up the same ladder he'd seen Izzy falling from when he entered the store. He wanted to take a closer look at the water damage in the wall.

"Look, I'm glad you're satisfying your curiosity, but I have a lot of things to do and don't have time to entertain you," snapped Isabel feeling anxious about her looming deadlines.

Sebastian looked down to see Izzy pacing. "What kind of things do you need to do for a dead-end bookstore?" asked Sebastian with more of a bite than he intended.

"Wow. Aren't you just a bowl of whipped cream with a cherry on top? I'm trying to get this place presentable before the parade next week," exclaimed Izzy. "And I'm hoping someone will stop by, see potential in the store and maybe they will buy it from Ms. Dottie and she won't have to worry about it."

Bash looked at Izzy with a quizzical brow. "Does Dottie even want to sell this place? It's been in her family for years."

Isabel hadn't taken time to ask Ms. Dottie about her future plans. She just hopped in her car and came when Dottie called and asked for help. She would do anything for the lady who took her into her heart and home a couple of years ago. Izzy just knew this store had once been a charming place to explore. She could feel it. It just needed a lot of elbow grease and maybe a new vision.

"Did you hear me Izzy?" asked Sebastian the second time. "I need to go find Asher and head back home."

"Oh sorry. I guess my mind was wandering off there for a minute."

Bash was at the door and turned before leaving, "I suppose

I'll be seeing you around."

"How's that?" She could feel the anxiety in the air. "I don't suppose our paths will be crossing much with you in Mobile and me in Fairhope."

"If only it were that easy," he replied as he closed the door, and the bell chimed a final ring.

Chapter 3

Isabel had been working day and night. The bookstore needed to be in tip top shape before the weekend of the Mystic Mutts of Revelry parade. She had to admit, Alabama had its own flare when it came to fundraisers. Izzy had never heard of a pet parade that raised funds to provide medical care and nutrition for homeless pets until they could be adopted. She was keen on getting the bookstore in prime condition before the day of the big event.

Izzy walked up the street with her morning coffee, greeting shop owners as she passed by, when she noticed a familiar male waiting for her at the door.

"Are you planning on greeting me every morning, Tristan?" she asked with a smile on her face.

"Oh, I was just passing by and saw this gift sitting in front of your door and thought I'd stand guard."

"A gift? From who?"

"Well, I didn't read the card. I just made sure no one took it," Tristan replied with a sheepish grin.

Izzy unlocked the door, sat down her coffee and took the gift that Tristan was holding. She opened it, slowly wondering who in the world could have left her a present. Inside the carefully wrapped package was a gift card to Camille's Café. The card inside read, "To help kick start your day, Your Secret Admirer." Obviously, someone knew she liked her morning coffee.

"So, what is it?" asked Tristan with a little too much enthusiasm. "Who's it from?"

"It says a Secret Admirer. And it's a gift card to Camille's Coffee Shop."

"It seems like someone knows your morning routine besides me," Tristan confirmed.

The thought of someone knowing her morning routine made her a little uneasy, but it was a small town. All you had to do was be on the street first thing in the morning and you would know her daily trek from her apartment to the coffee shop to the bookstore. It didn't take a rocket scientist.

The bell rang indicating that the first customer of the day was arriving. Izzy turned around in time to see Bash walking in carrying tools, paint brushes and rollers. One look at Tristan standing so close to her and the hair on the back of his neck began to bristle.

"Uh…hello. I mean good morning," she greeted him trying to be enthusiastic. "What are you doing here and with all that…

stuff?"

"I noticed when I was looking over the place the other day that lots of work needs to be done and thought you could definitely use a hand."

Tristan was growing impatient with this new guy that was interrupting his alone time with Izzy. This had become their morning routine over the past month and now this guy was intruding. Frustrated, he said a quick goodbye, gave Izzy a hug, then left to begin his day at the hardware store.

"What are you doing here?" came the immediate accusatory tone from Izzy.

"You know about a week ago, I could have sworn I saw you sitting on the bench above the bluff looking out at the bay. This girl looked just like you and I remembered how much you enjoyed just sitting and looking out at the water. Of course, I had no idea you were living anywhere near here, so I chalked it up to an active imagination," he turned around to make sure she was listening.

"At first, I just glanced but the girl looked so much like you that I had to get a better look. There was no reason to believe it was you, but I couldn't shake the feeling. I ran up to my office to find my binoculars."

"Wait, what are you talking about?" Izzy stopped him mid-story. "What office?"

"I'll get to that. The phone was ringing when I made it upstairs. Someone was looking to charter a sailboat. By the time I finished the order and looked again, the girl was gone. Just vanished into thin air. town. All you had to do was be on the street first thing in the morning and you would know her daily ever as vivid as that day. Now I look back and wonder if it really was you I saw sitting there."

She sighed, "I sit on that bench most afternoons after working in the bookstore all day. I let the breeze from the bay wash the stress off of me. And I love to hear the water hit against the pier, see the children running around and watch the parents take pictures," Izzy glanced at Bash. "Sometimes I just walk on the pier and look at the fish and sea gulls. It's really relaxing after a long day...wait, what did you say about an office?"

Sebastian couldn't help but smile. "A lot has happened since we parted, Iz. I wanted to make some changes in my life, so I left the corporate world behind." Bash looked like a little boy on Christmas morning. "I bought a small private marina at the mouth of Rock Creek. It's just a stone's throw away from here. I knew I couldn't compete with the Yacht Club so I decided my place would be a little different." She could feel his excitement about this new adventure from the brightness in his eyes and the elated tone of his voice.

"I provide a place where the locals can dock their sailboats at a more reasonable price than the bigger marinas. I'm working on an idea where boat owners can rent their boats out, similar to an Airbnb, just on a boat. Guests can spend the night on the sailboat at the marina or there could be charters where the owners add that on as an extra charge. I'd like for my role to be as a broker. I own the marina and rent slips, I watch out for the owner's boats or could rent them out for charters as well as an Airbnb. It's still in the planning stages right now. I like the quaintness of a small marina, but I believe to be successful you have to keep looking ahead. Changing with the times."

Isabel sat and listened to Bash pour out his vision and heart. His passion and excitement were so evident. For a brief moment, she fought the desire to reach out and give him a big hug.

"I'm ecstatic for you Bash. All I've ever wanted was for you to be happy." She found herself fumbling with the gift card she'd recently received.

"So now Tristan is bringing you presents?" Bash couldn't help but notice the unwrapped gift on the front counter.

"Apparently I have a secret admirer," Izzy replied with a smug look on her face.

"Really? Let me see." Bash had taken the card out of her hand and read it before she could stop him.

Grabbing the card out of his hand, Izzy continued, "what did you say you were doing here?"

"I've come to help get this place ready for the re-opening."

"That's nice of you, and unexpected, but I think I've got it covered," replied Izzy.

"I'm sure you do. Where should I start painting first?"

"Look," snapped Isabel. "Just because we were cordial the other day doesn't mean things are all warm and fuzzy between us now."

"If I was after warm and fuzzy, I'd get a puppy," countered Sebastian as he picked up his supplies heading for the first hole to be spackled. "No, I firmly believe you and I are going to find our way back to one another Iz. I'm just giving you time to get use to the idea."

His sheer obstinance was irritating. She knew he cared for her. She knew she cared for him. But sometimes that's just not enough.

Chapter 4

Izzy could hardly believe opening day of Bayfront Books had finally arrived. The streets were buzzing with people from town as well as those that were visiting, just as she imagined it would be. The weekend was full of Mardi Gras parades and the afternoon showcase was the Mystic Mutt Revelry parade.

The bookstore had been cleaned, dusted, swept, patched and painted. The window displays were adorned with sparkly green, gold and purple draping. Beads had been strung throughout the room to create the full Mardi Gras flare. Even beignets graced the counter for the customers who would be passing through.

Izzy had hired a part time girl who could help with the register when she needed to tend to the accounts and inventory. Olivia was a bubbly girl, in her early 20s who went to college in Mobile a couple of days a week. If she wasn't at school, you could usually find her at the bookstore. She loved books just like Isabel and was contemplating journalism as her major. Izzy hoped the exposure to the bookstore would be a perfect time for her to reflect and decide what she would like to do with her future.

Tristan appeared in the doorway right on time as planned. He wanted to take her to the parade and introduce her to this fun tradition in the town while spending the rest of the day in her company. Izzy straightened up a few more things in the store before grabbing a light jacket and following Tristan out to the sidewalk. They arrived just in time to see the first wagon pass by.

The theme of the Mystic Mutt parade was "Pirates and Pups." Isabel erupted in laughter as soon as she saw some of the creative costumes the owners had designed. The first wagon was decorated like a pirate boat and carrying a German Shepherd. It's hard to take a dog seriously when he has a cardboard sword strapped around his body and a pirate hat attached to his head. Some dogs were outfitted with patches on their eyes and smaller pups could be found riding in a wagon, dressed in glitzy gold and placed in a treasure chest. It was definitely something to see if you were ever nearby.

Izzy and Tristan wove their way through the crowd taking in all the sights and sounds. Street shops had their doors swung open hoping to entice any curious customers to come inside. Water bowls had been placed at the entrance to the stores for all the thirsty pets passing by and a big jar of treats could be taken at the pet owners' discretion. It was electric with excitement and Isabel couldn't remember the last time she had laughed so hard or had so much fun.

Everyone in town knew Tristan. Of course, he had lived in Fairhope his whole life. They were greeted fondly at every turn and Tristan made sure to introduce Izzy to all his friends. He even bought her cotton candy. Not quite Mardi Gras food, but Izzy wasn't fond of the much-coveted Moon Pies that most people fought over.

"Would you like to go out to din...." started Tristan, but he was quickly interrupted when they ran smack dab into Sebastian.

"I've been looking everywhere for you Iz" came the greeting. "Olivia told me you were out here somewhere."

"Looks like you found me," came the irritated response.

"Well, if your good friend here is done parading you around," Bash couldn't help but smile at his wittiness, "I have something else I'd like to show you. Oh, and Olivia said she needed you back at the store when you were finished."

Izzy was conflicted about what to do. If she left with Bash, Tristan would think she was ditching him. However, the store was the most important issue at hand. Before she could respond, Tristan suggested she go ahead and leave.

"Explain to me how you seem to be everywhere. Every time I turn around, there you are." Izzy snapped even though Bash didn't seem to be listening. He reached back and grabbed her hand and told her to hold on. They were weaving in and out of people along the sidewalk. Animals were everywhere and Izzy had to keep looking down in order not to trip over even the smallest of pets. By the time they reached the front of the bookstore, Isabel was totally out of breath.

"You're welcome," smiled Sebastian.

"For what?"

"Getting you away from your personal tour guide and delivering you to the store in record time."

She shut her eyes a moment trying to clear up the murk that was clouding her brain.

"This…you…just showing up… it's awkward. And just plain weird."

"Why?" asked Sebastian rather perplexed.

"Why? WHY? Because we have a history. We were together at one time. You do realize that everyone in this small town is talking! They probably think we are together again." Isabel's voice had reached an irritating pitch.

"I don't think anyone in this small town even knows who we are, or cares. And even if they did, so what?"

Isabel was fighting for a rational argument. "Well, maybe I want to date someone else around here and you're in the way?"

Bash took a step back, annoyance written all over his face.

"Tristan? Is that who you want to date?"

Izzy responded in frustration, "okay, forget that. I don't want to date anyone. I just don't want people talking about me, or about us. I'm going inside now to see what Olivia needs."

As she entered the bookstore, she couldn't help but see Olivia sporting a girlish grin and pointing to the big bouquet of wildflowers sitting on the counter. Izzy walked over and picked up the card that was

attached. The card read, "You're as pretty as the wildflowers you pick in the morning, Signed, Your Secret Admirer."

Izzy didn't say a word, put the card on the counter and walked to the back. Bash and Liv picked up the card to see what it said. They exchanged an awkward glance not fulling understanding what had upset Isabel so much that she left the room. When she returned carrying a vase full of wildflowers, they quickly made the connection. She sat them down next to the others on the counter and the bouquets were nearly identical.

"At first I thought it was really sweet to have a secret admirer." She stared at the bouquets. "You know, maybe it was from a sweet young boy who had visited the store. Or a customer I had helped find a book. Or maybe someone who just wanted to be nice. But now I'm starting to think that my secret admirer is watching me, and it would appear he's watching me very closely."

Chapter 5

Isabel needed some fresh air and a few minutes alone before Olivia joined her and they left for dinner. It was nice having a girl around, even if she was several years younger. Olivia always acted mature for her age and now more than ever Izzy enjoyed her company and having someone to talk to.

The bay was especially beautiful tonight. The water was a little rough which might explain the cool breeze Izzy was enjoying as the wind whipped off the water. Olivia soon joined her and suggested they hit up a food truck that sat next to a small marina. They could enjoy eating outside by the bay and take advantage of a beautiful evening. Izzy agreed and off they went.

Isabel had never been outside of town. Ever since she'd arrived, she had been working or sleeping. All of that took place in the same spot. Of course, there were short trips to the grocery store but that was at the edge of town in the other direction. Olivia must have been to this place before because she rounded the curves on the road with familiarity.

Upon arriving, Izzy fell in love with the area immediately.

Outside lights were strung back and forth between the big oak trees creating a canopy over all the picnic tables. Lounge chairs and fire pits were spread throughout creating intimate sitting areas. A small marina was nestled beside the awesome grassy space and was decked out with sparkly lights that bounced off the water. It made the whole area feel cozy.

The food truck, Buck's Burgers, was hopping and if the line was any indication of how good the food was, they were in for a treat. Olivia offered to stand in line while Izzy took a tour of the area. The lounging chairs were in groups surrounding a fire pit. It didn't matter if they were lit or not because just the setting invited conversation. She wandered throughout the space until her path ended at the bay. It truly was a beautiful evening. The sun had yet to set and the glow on the water exuded peaceful-ness. It was just what Isabel needed.

Laughter could be heard wafting down from above, causing her to whip around and see the culprit who was interrupting her serene moment. It didn't take long to identify the three figures standing on the balcony overlooking the marina. Surely her eyes were playing tricks on her. Could that really be Sebastian, Emma and Asher? Before she could step back into the shadows, in an attempt not to be noticed, Bash looked down and locked eyes with her. The look on his face said it all and Isabel saw him quickly retreat.

Thinking that was a good idea, she walked, or rather power walked up the hill back towards the food truck scanning the crowd for any sign of Olivia. Once she spotted her sitting on the far end of the lounge area, her feet couldn't move quick enough to join her friend. She had just arrived, out of breath, when a familiar voice broke the silence.

"Hi Iz. Hi Liv," said Bash. "Glad ya'll are here."

"What did that mean?" thought Izzy. He didn't invite us. He didn't know we were coming. And from the looks of things, he already had a small party going on himself. Isabel just grunted a greeting and sat down to devour her burger. Oliva being her bubbly self, talked a mile a minute about everything under the sun. Izzy wondered if Olivia sensed the tension that hung in the air. That's something she would ask at a later time.

"This is the marina I told you about Iz. I've been dying to show it to you, but you've been so busy with the store I didn't want to invite you just yet." Sebastian was trying to weigh Izzy's temperament knowing she had seen Emma upstairs with he and Asher.

"I was just," Bash started then corrected himself. "We were just getting ready to take my boat out for an early evening ride. I'd love for you both to join us."

Before Izzy could utter a word, Olivia was practically jumping up and hugging him. Something about loving boats and wishing she had one and what a beautiful night for an evening on the water. Izzy could sit there like the pouting ex-girlfriend, everyone wondering if she was really over Bash, or she could go along and not make a fuss.

By the time the boat was loaded with all the passengers, there wasn't going to be much light left. Asher gave Iz a warm hug when he saw her, but Emma's greeting was a tad more formal. Isabel didn't care because there was no love lost between the two of them. Bash had also invited the young guy who worked for him, Chance, to join the group. As he put it, "why don't you come along and keep Liv' company." Thank goodness it was too dark to tell if either of them blushed.

Isabel, Liv and Chance sat towards the back of the boat while the girls finished their dinner. Asher, Emma and Bash had already eaten and were busy in conversation as the boat skidded along. The water was smooth as glass and Izzy had to admit there was nothing she liked more than to be out on the water. She closed her eyes, let the wind blow in her face and did her best to just relax.

Bash pulled the boat into a small cove wanting to drop anchor so they could float for a bit. He asked Chance to go to the front of the boat to help guide him to the perfect spot. As the boat came to a stop Bash solicited Asher to go to the back and drop anchor. It was sitting right at Izzy's feet. Frustrated he might be implying she wasn't capable of helping out, she informed him she could easily take care of the anchor and reached down to grab it. It wasn't heavy but the rope was slightly knotted. Isabel stepped to the side of the boat and wound up to throw the anchor overboard, before realizing the rope was tangled around her ankles. Between the heaviness of the anchor and the entanglement of the rope, Izzy lost her balance and went over the side, anchor and all.

Everyone stared at the ripple in the water where she had entered. Knowing Bash wouldn't let anyone on his boat without a life jacket, they knew she would eventually surface. Sputtering water and wiping the hair away from her face, she soon appeared from the darkened pool.

"So, I was just wondering," said Bash with no attempt to hide his sarcasm, "if you were still capable all on your own or would you like a little help getting back in the boat?"

Izzy was still muttering under her breath as she sat in the back of the boat trying to hide her embarrassment from the rest of the group. Stubbornness had often been the downfall of her decisions. She gazed out at the bay in deep thought as they made their way back to the shore.

"I don't know what that was all about back there," said Bash as he helped her out of the boat. "But there's *still* nothing going on between me and Emma. We're just friends."

Emma had been a part of the equation before when Izzy couldn't decide whether to trust Sebastian enough to date him. They were connected. She was a significant part of his past and apparently still a part of his present.

"I'm not interested in a discussion. I don't want to debate or rehash anything right now. We can be friends, or you can push until we're not. That's up to you," Isabel nipped as she stepped onto dry land.

She turned and left Bash standing alone. Grabbing Olivia by the hand, she pulled her along until they finally reached the car. Izzy hoped to be gone as quickly as they had arrived.

Chapter 6

There were many days it took longer than it should for Isabel to make the walk from Camille's Café to the bookstore. Anyone who knew her well realized she wasn't much of a morning person and not to talk to her until she'd had her first cup of coffee. This morning she had added a sugary delight to her morning routine and was munching on a blueberry muffin as she strolled along. Even from a distance Izzy could make out the silhouette of Tristan James standing outside the bookstore waiting for her. Was this becoming a daily habit?

Since the store renovations had been completed, she wasn't seeing him every day. Izzy hadn't made a trip to the hardware store in weeks and Tristan had no excuses to make a daily visit. Yet here he stood in front of the bookstore waiting on her.

"Morning Tristan," greeted Izzy as she got within speaking distance.

"Morning Izzy," came the cheery reply. "I just realized I hadn't seen you in a while, unless you count seeing you the other night when Olivia dropped you off."

"Oh yeah," she replied with a confused look on her face. "But I didn't see you the other night, did I?"

"Oh...I guess not," he stammered, looking a bit uncomfortable. "I meant I was running some errands and saw Olivia drop you off. It looked like you had just stepped out of a shower, but with all your clothes on," Tristan responded with a nervous chuckle.

"I fell in the bay," Izzy laughed in spite of herself, still feeling the sting of total embarrassment. "We were out with Bash on his boat and I tried to throw out the anchor, but the anchor held on."

"Oh, so you were out with Sebastian the other night?" asked Tristan.

"We, as in a group of people, went out on Bash's boat," explained Isabel. "It was an impromptu invite and I fell in the water. Story over." Izzy opened the door and walked inside with Tristan following close behind.

"I picked this up for you this morning," Tristan handed her an envelope. "I found it laying in front of the door when I arrived."

Olivia had just arrived for the day and saw Tristan hovering around Isabel. "What are you guys doing?" she said in a bright and cheery tone. Olivia Barton was the epitome of a morning person. Isabel loved her new friend so much she tried not to let it annoy her.

"Tristan found an envelope outside the door this morning," answered Izzy.

"Well, open it!" exclaimed Olivia. "Let's see if it's something else from your secret admirer."

"You have a secret admirer?" asked Tristan with a quizzical look on his face. "I thought I was the only secret admirer you had."

Isabel turned around trying to hide her schoolgirl blushing over Tristan's comment. Opening the envelope, she slid out the contents. It was an 8x10 photo of herself, sitting on her favorite bench behind the bookstore, staring out at the bay. The card read, "When you're as pretty as a picture, someone should capture the moment. Signed, Your Secret Admirer."

"Wow, that's a beautiful picture of you Izzy," observed Tristan. "You should think about framing it." He gave her a smile and wink, then left the girls to start their day.

"I know Tristan is nice and all," said Liv, "but he kind of creeps me out sometimes. And what was up with you the other night in the boat?"

"I haven't known Tristan that long, but he seems alright," replied Isabel. "As far as the other night, I was just being stupid. When I saw Emma at Bash's apartment it brought up all my past insecurities."

"He picked you before Isabel, not Emma." Olivia had been

filled in on all the romantic twists in Izzy's past. They had one long girls' night and Izzy had laid it all out: her and Asher dated in high school; Sebastian and Emma had dated when they were younger, but Emma still pined for him all these years later. Asher and Sebastian had been best friends since middle school, but Izzy never liked Sebastian when she dated Asher. However, when she ran into Bash years later when she moved to Mobile, he had worked his charm on her and they dated for a year. A classic tale of love and all its triangles: it's what good romance novels are written about.

The girls weren't too far apart in age and had developed a close friendship fairly quick. Olivia knew Izzy still had feelings for Bash, whether she admitted it to herself or not. She watched her friend walk to the back knowing she was headed for her office. Anytime Sebastian showed up or his name came up, she could still see the pain in Isabel's eyes.

"Hey pretty girl," came the cheery greeting from the front door. Chance was all smiles when Olivia turned to see him entering the bookstore.

"Well, hey yourself," replied Olivia. She could hardly contain her excitement upon seeing the handsome young man who had joined them for the boat ride at Bash's marina. "What brings you in?"

"Two things really," Chance said leaning over the counter to get closer to the girl who had caught his eye. "One, I wanted to see if you had plans for Friday night. Two, I was looking for my boss who said he was stopping by here."

"Good job of asking me out first," giggled a beaming Olivia. "I would love to go out with you Friday night. And Sebastian hasn't been by as of yet."

Chance and Olivia discussed their plans for Friday night, their two grinning faces leaning in close. The love bug was circling Fairhope and there was no telling who would be bitten next.

<h1 style="text-align:center">Chapter 7</h1>

Several customers were in the store a few hours later when Sebastian walked in with determination written all over his face. He was on a mission, and he wasn't going to let anyone or anything get in his way.

"Where's she at?" he asked looking directly at Liv.

"Where do you think?" she answered, directing her gaze towards the back of the store.

Bash headed towards the back where Izzy had set up an office when she arrived in Fairhope. It was small, musty and smelled like old books. A tiny desk sat in the corner that was just big enough to hold a computer. The only positive characteristic in the room was the view of the bay through the back window. Izzy was staring intently at the computer screen when Sebastian walked in.

"Are you ready?" he asked as if they had been preparing for this moment for weeks.

Izzy didn't turn around, "I have no idea what you're talking about."

"We're going out. You and me. For the day."

"I have too many things on my plate right now Sebastian, and the last thing I want to do is go anywhere with you," she answered completely uninterested in whatever game he was trying to play.

"I wasn't asking," Bash responded. "We can do this the easy way, walk out like two adults ready for a nice day, or we can do it the hard way."

"Like I said, I'm not interested." Isabel got up to retrieve a water bottle from the small fridge she had bought for the office.

Sebastian sighed realizing this was going to happen the hard way. He blocked her path, picked her up and threw her over his shoulder.

"Put me down Sebastian," she whispered indignantly throughout the bookstore as he carted her out. People are looking! This is my place of business and you are embarrassing me."

"I offered to do it the easy way and you wouldn't cooperate," declared Sebastian. "Liv, she's going out for the day, please lock up when you leave this evening." Olivia waved, gave Iz a thumbs up with a sheepish grin as they exited the building.

Isabel was mortified at the display that was taking place. Customers in the store were trying to stifle their snickering while people on the street were staring and whispering.

"Are you trying to run the business completely in the

ground?" she snapped as Bash sat her down in the front seat of his truck.

As he reached over to snap her seat belt in place, he gave her a firm stare. "You can get out and run but I'm just going to come in and do it all over again. You've been working for weeks now renovating this place, trying to balance the books and see if you can turn this store around. You need a day off to relax and so do I."

Isabel knew he meant what he said and if she returned to the bookstore, he would just embarrass her further. She sat still, steaming. She may go along for now, but she had no intention of relaxing.

Refusing to make small talk, she stared out the window. Izzy had to admit, Fairhope was a beautiful small town, and she hadn't spent nearly enough time enjoying the scenery. They drove to the outskirts of the area before the truck slowed down and turned onto a dirt road outlined with big oak trees. The sign read "Double Oak Farm."

Curiosity got the better of her, so she broke the silence. "Where are we? Isn't this like a wedding venue?"

Before Bash could answer, the truck pulled up in front of a farmhouse where an attractive lady in her forties was waiting out front. He walked up and gave her a big ol' southern hug as if they were distant relatives. It looked as if she was giving him directions and handed him something. Isabel couldn't see what it was. As she waited in the truck, she could see the lady trying to peer around Bash to get a better look at her. She gave Izzy a little wave as she turned around to go back to the house.

Isabel was confused, intrigued and a little miffed. Why was this lady grinning at her? Did she think she was one of Sebastian's many girls? Was this part of his routine? Why didn't he introduce her? A whirlwind of questions spun around in her mind as Bash made his way back to the truck.

"Just give me a second, before you start grilling me," he smiled and ducked as if Izzy might slug him. "That's Georgia. She and her husband Bill own this place. They've become good friends of mine and have helped me with some ideas for the marina." He paused as if he were in deep thought. "They were the first to dock their boat at my place. My first customers. We swap ideas and help each other out sometimes. They are typically closed today, but Georgia is doing me a favor."

"Well, she was checking me out like a hawk circling a dead animal."

"She was teasing me about whether there was actually anyone in the truck." Bash couldn't help but laugh. "I always come out here by myself. She said I was just making up having a girlfriend." Izzy shot him a look.

"Had a girlfriend..." Bash muttered. They both stared out

their windows, trying to ignore the awkward mistake.

Sebastian pulled the truck around to the back of the farm, past the barn where the venue hosted parties, weddings, and small concerts. On the other side was an open field with a stage at one end. Izzy had heard of the outdoor concerts in the former pecan orchard and was looking forward to going one day when the weather turned cooler.

The land was gorgeous. There was a stable at the end of the drive and Izzy saw some little ponies and a few full-grown horses. They were so pretty in the field, grazing. She loved riding horses. Her grandparents had owned property in Arkansas, and she had learned to ride at a young age. She often thought of her grandma and grandpa and the good times she had on their farm. She remembered how they would stand outside, wiping tears as they waved goodbye, and would watch the car all the way down the lane until it turned onto the main road. Those were cherished memories for Izzy.

Sebastian startled her when he opened the truck door then guided her towards two horses in the corral already saddled. Izzy looked at Bash and he was smugly grinning like he always does when he is happy with himself.

"I don't want company. And I'm not looking to be anyone's company today," stated Isabel.

"Then we'll just ride in silence. But we are going to ride, Iz," replied Sebastian.

"I am surprised you even know how to saddle a horse," came the sarcastic response.

"I have put on a saddle or two, for your information," he shot her a defiant look. "But Georgia was kind enough to have them saddled for us."

Izzy wasn't going to give him the satisfaction of knowing how much she really needed this. In spite of basically kidnapping and embarrassing her, she was going to try to relax and enjoy the day. She really did need a day off.

"Nice North Face backpack, John Wayne," said Isabel grinning as Bash returned from the truck with it slung over his shoulder.

"I missed that," replied Bash.

"Missed what?"

"Your smile. You've been holding back until now."

Isabel looked at Bash feeling self-conscious that he could still make her blush.

"So, which one do you want?" asked Sebastian, letting Isabel take her time looking the horses over. Both were mature and looked easy going. One was brown with a lighter color mane and tail. The other one was jet black and shiny.

"I'll take the black one and leave the brown one for you. Besides, the light mane looks like it's dyed blonde, and we know how you love your blondes!" Izzy laughed.

"That joke is really getting old," replied Bash, rolling his eyes.

Isabel mounted the horse with little effort. "So, where's the trail we follow?"

"When they have a paying group here, they ride down by the creek and through the orchard," replied Bash. "I thought it would be nice going on our own trail."

They rode slowly, getting used to the horses and being in the saddle. The smell of the well-worn leather couldn't be mistaken and creaked as they rode along. The orchard was beautiful, and they rode in silence heading towards a strand of trees at the far end of the field.

"You know Iz, most of these horses are rescues. Bill and Georgia started the farm as a concert place and wedding venue, but they love animals too," Bash explained as they rode along. "Oh, that's right, you don't want company." He shot her a look to see her response.

"It's okay to talk about your friends," she replied, not making eye contact.

"Well, they heard about several horses that had been rescued across the county, so they contacted the animal shelter about housing the horses. The local shelter is only equipped for small animals, so they didn't have a place for the horses to stay. Bill offered his land and a very beneficial relationship developed. If the shelter needs to keep a horse, they bring it here. It's fed, has medical treatment, and is taken care of until the animal is ready to be adopted. And as you can see, sometimes they just keep them."

"Your taste in friends seems to be improving," she gave him a lazy smile. "They sound like amazing people, and these horses are certainly taken care of." Izzy reached down and stroked her horse's neck.

"They were worried about their temperament after being abused and neglected. Some are not well suited for group rides and others are just plain mean, sort of like some girls I know!" Sebastian winked at Izzy and nudged his horse into a run.

Not wanting to be left behind, soon she was galloping across the field. The horses reached a pace where the ride smoothed out. They seemed to be enjoying the freedom to run, and no urging was needed from the riders.

As they neared the grove of trees, Sebastian eased back on the reins and watched as Izzy slowed to a gallop. She gasped when she saw the change in the landscape. The trees grew along a little creek, no more than 20 feet wide. The water was dark, almost tea colored. It was the tannic water of so many of the creeks in the south. It was captivating how the land had changed elevation. There was a ten-foot drop and a perfect tiny waterfall that had formed where the creek dropped off the ledge. The water gurgled gently while birds and fish haunted the shallows of the creek.

The oaks and bay trees formed a perfect canopy. Only a stray beam of sunlight made it to the ground. The shade kept the vegetation from growing, so the ground looked like a carpet of mulch. Izzy was still taking in the sights when Sebastian caught up.

"It looks like you found my little piece of heaven," Sebastian said in almost a hush. "Isn't it beautiful?"

"How did you find it?"

"I would love to take credit, but Bill showed it to me," admitted Bash. "I come here when I need to get away. The bay is beautiful, but this is another kind of beauty, especially in the fall when the leaves are turning."

They dismounted their horses and tied the reigns to a cable that stretched between two oaks. A short walk led them down by the creek where they found the perfect spot to sit and take in the atmosphere around them. Sebastian spread the blanket beneath one of the big bay trees. The aroma of the trees and the oak leaves created a unique and enticing aroma. The mere ambiance would slow your heart rate and lower your blood pressure.

"I know you're not a wine person, but this is just one of those days Iz." He pulled out a bottle and two glasses from his backpack.

"Where is it?" asked Izzy with a smidge of sarcasm. "You know, the tree with the notches for all the girls you've brought down here".

"There's not a tree that's big enough," smirked Sebastian trying to keep himself from laughing.

Izzy couldn't help but laugh herself. He looked over to catch her eye. When she stopped laughing, she could see that Bash was staring at her. Izzy's stomach tightened into knots. Bash moved closer, never taking his eyes from hers. He brushed the hair away from her face and leaned over to kiss her. Without warning, Isabel made a quick move and Sebastian nearly landed flat on his face. It was hard to tell if he was more surprised or embarrassed.

"I can't Bash. Not now," replied Izzy as she looked away trying to hide her emotions.

"I thought about coming and staying at your place today. Forcing you to sit down and talk this through with me, even if it took all night."

"You can't force me to talk now, Bash. You wouldn't listen to me before when you broke it off with me!"

"We are going to talk, Isabel. Sooner or later. But today's not the day."

"I'm not here for your convenience Sebastian," she shot him a blank stare.

"There's nothing convenient about you Iz." Bash leaned over again and this time she didn't pull away. He kissed her softly at first and then kissed her with the same passion they had once shared as a couple. Isabel finally pulled away before she lost her nerve to keep him at a safe distance.

"And there's nothing convenient about that," whispered Bash as their eyes met once again. "We won't hash it out today, but we will talk it out soon."

They sat in silence for quite some time enjoying the sights and sounds that were all around them. By the time Bash stood to pack things away, some of the stress had vanished from Izzy's face. He reached down to help her up, folded the blanket and put everything away. As he swung his horse toward the barn, he pointed to a lone cedar tree a few feet away. "That's the tree with the notches."

Izzy squinted straining to see, "But I don't see any notches."

"Exactly! Giddy-up Blondie!" Bash was laughing as he galloped off toward the barn with Izzy following close behind.

Chapter 8

Once they returned to town, Sebastian and Izzy found a small diner open down the street from the bookstore. It had been a relaxing day of riding and enjoying nature, but it had left them famished. Their sunny day had turned into a sunset glow; the perfect ending to a great time together. It was strange to feel so close and yet so far apart from someone you once loved. While sitting inside the cozy diner, enjoying some good ol' southern comfort food, a black cloud had started to form outside. What should have been a peaceful end to a relaxing day turned into a mad dash for shelter from the pelting rain.

By the time they reached the awning in front of the store, Isabel and Bash were soaking wet. When they finally caught their breath, they did a quick survey of one another. Laughter broke out and could be heard echoing down the deserted street. Sebastian intuitively reached up and tucked a wet piece of hair behind Izzy's ear. The brush of his hand against her cheek sent her heart racing, and she knew it wasn't because of the sprint to the store. Isabel's hand was shaking as she struggled to unlock the door so they could shelter inside. Bash gently took the key from her hand and unlocked the door. The bookstore was dark and quiet. Water was dripping from their clothes and both fought the urge to look into one another's eyes.

"I think you should get out of those wet clothes before you get sick," said Sebastian with a sly smile and wink.

"You'll never change," replied Izzy, grinning in spite of herself. "Thank you for forcing me to have some fun today."

Sebastian quickly turned and left before he said something that would scare her away. Today's outing had broken down some walls, and he didn't want to do anything that would mess that up. He was halfway down the street when he realized he still had the store keys in his hand. Running back in the pouring rain, Bash opened the door and headed upstairs to Izzy's apartment. He found her standing in the doorway, frozen in place. His smile quickly faded when he glanced inside the apartment door.

The flat had been ransacked. Papers were strewn all over the floor and the two antique chairs that sat on either side of the couch had been knocked over. The drawers from the bedroom dresser were open with her personal belongings hanging out. What the perpetrator was looking for was anyone's guess. Sebastian took Isabel's hand and led her to the couch, concerned she might faint.

"Why…why would someone do this?" mumbled Isabel in shock.

"I don't know Iz," replied Sebastian looking around the room, "but we need to call the police."

When the cops arrived, they went through the basic formality of questions you would ask after a break in: Had Isabel noticed any strangers loitering around the store? Were there people asking questions that seemed out of place? Had anything been stolen? Isabel couldn't put a complete sentence together, let alone remember anything that was helpful.

The police dusted for fingerprints, examined how the intruder had entered the apartment and checked the store downstairs before they left. Nothing appeared to be out of place, no money was missing. The police found no evidence of what the intruder might have been looking for.

Bash poured Izzy a glass of water and brought it to her while he cleaned up the mess. She was still shaking when he finally sat down beside her on the couch.

"Would you stay with me tonight, Sebastian?" asked Isabel in almost a whisper.

"Of course I will," he replied. "I think my clothes are finally dry."

Izzy disappeared into the bathroom and took a good look at herself in the mirror. Her hair had finally dried from the pouring rain and makeup was smeared under her eyes. The claw foot bathtub that Ms. Dottie had brought in especially for her was calling her name. What she wouldn't give for a long bubble bath right now. However, Sebastian had so graciously said he would stay and she didn't want to take the time to relax while she had company.

When she returned, she was wearing flannel pajama bottoms and a t-shirt. Sebastian couldn't help but notice how pretty she was regardless of what she was wearing. Her long brown hair had been gathered into a ponytail and ringlets framed her face. Sebastian watched as she crossed the room. She was quiet as if the very breath had been knocked out of her. He'd always admired her strength, but now she looked so tiny, frail and defeated. He wanted to wrap his arms around her. He would do anything to make her feel safe, but their recent past kept him planted on the sofa.

Isabel went to the closet, retrieved a pillow and blanket then handed them to Sebastian. She assured him the couch would be a comfortable bed before climbing into her own hoping to erase all that had transpired over the last few hours.

How long Izzy tossed and turned she didn't know. It seemed like an eternity. Eventually she turned on the radio hoping to drown out the memories of her safe haven being ransacked just hours before.

"Bash?" whispered Isabel. "Are you asleep?"

"No Iz. I was waiting for you to fall asleep first."

"Would you mind…would it be too much if I asked you to come lay by me?" asked Izzy in such a quiet voice Sebastian wasn't sure he heard her correctly.

Bash turned towards the bed to see if he was hearing things. "Did you ask me to lay down beside you?"

"I'm sorry Sebastian…" answered Isabel with a slight quiver in her voice. She turned over once again and gave her pillow a sturdy punch. "I shouldn't have asked you. I'm just trembling and feel…"

Izzy felt a presence beside her and looked up to see Bash standing by her bed with pillow and blanket in hand. This wasn't exactly what he had in mind by getting closer to Isabel. She looked like a terrified child after tonight's events and his only desire was to make sure she felt safe. He smoothed down the comforter and laid down on top. The two of them laid there, perfectly still, hoping the melody ringing out over the radio would mask the turmoil they felt within. Then, as if on que, Sebastian wrapped his arm around Izzy and pulled her close. She nestled in and quietly cried until she finally lulled herself to sleep. Sebastian laid there awake for quite some time breathing in the scent that can only be provided by Isabel Porter.

Chapter 9

It had been a few days since the break in when Izzy woke up to find Bash in the kitchen making breakfast. After overcoming the first night of sheer terror, she repeatedly told him she was fine, and he could go back to his own place. This was now a recurring theme every day, and always ended with the same resolve.

"We need some ground rules," Izzy said as she walked into the kitchen and poured herself a cup of coffee.

"Fine. Write me up a list," Bash replied as he wrapped up the breakfast sandwich he'd made and headed for the door. "I made one for you if you want it."

"You can't just come in here and take over," replied Izzy, frustration written all over her face.

"Okay, put that at the top of your list," Bash countered as if he wasn't really listening.

"You need to respect my privacy and realize I don't need someone hovering over me every night," Izzy explained while nervously following him around the apartment.

"Uh huh," Bash responded as he paused at the door. "Somebody broke into your apartment, Iz. Regardless of what's happened between us in the past, I'm not going to let anything happen to you now. I promised Ms. Dottie. So, we both have to deal with that." He looked as cornered as she felt. "Once the police make some progress, then we'll discuss it. And for the record, you might think because of the way things turned out between us, you don't matter to me. You'd be wrong. Now lock your door after I leave." Sebastian grabbed his jacket and was out the door before Izzy could counter with a response.

He knew there needed to be rules, or guidelines anyway. There was right and there was wrong, and a big mass of gray in between. It was okay if she wanted to set up some rules, as long as Izzy understood he'd be exploring the gray as much as he could.

Isabel didn't have time to dwell on her latest exchange with Bash. There were too many items on her to-do list to get ready for the crowd coming to the Arts & Crafts Festival planned over the weekend. It was one of the biggest festivals of the year in Fairhope. Besides having the bookstore open, Izzy decided to take some of the older books she had found boxed up in the back and have a vintage book sale. It would help clean the clutter out of the store and interest avid readers like herself who might be looking for old books they couldn't find otherwise. Izzy had rented a tent and would run the booth outside while Olivia ran the bookstore. It could mean double the money in one day, but the idea was solely in her head now, and she needed to make it a reality.

Once Olivia arrived at work, Isabel discussed the plan for the day and all the things she needed to check off her list. She had just reached the door when Bash came bolting in and nearly knocked her down.

"Seriously, you just left," snapped Isabel.

"I forgot my wallet," he replied and dashed up the stairs.

Izzy turned to see a grin spread across Olivia's face. "Do you have something you want to share, Iz?" asked her newfound friend who could hardly contain her schoolgirl excitement.

"No. I don't," she mumbled. "And wipe that girlish grin off your face." Izzy couldn't believe she was having to explain this ridiculous situation to anyone. let alone her friend.

"Oh, before I forget," Liv reached under the counter and produced a gift bag, "I found this in front of the store when I arrived this morning."

Since Bash had been staying at her place, there had been no need to make a trip to Camille's for coffee each morning. It was always ready and waiting. She hadn't been taking her morning walks and forgot about the gifts that were being left in front of the store.

"Oooo, did Chance give you something pretty?" sang Bash as he entered the room.

"Uhhh no," responded Olivia. "Why? Is he getting me something pretty? Tell me Bash. You know something, I know you do." He looked like a mouse caught in a trap. Chance and Olivia had been dating ever since the night they met on the boat. Sebastian tried to gradually sneak out the door until he realized the gift must be for Isabel.

"So, whose sending you gifts?" asked Bash trying to hide his displeasure.

"I'd love to tell you, but I have no idea," she replied nonchalantly. "I've been receiving gifts off and on for the past few weeks from a secret admirer." She smiled as if to say, "Look what you missed out on."

"Hmm...let's see what you got," he said, trying to seem uninterested, but Izzy knew better.

She untied the ribbon on the bag and pulled out a box. Inside was a huge chocolate heart that had been broken in half. The card read, "You held my heart...then you broke it, Your Secret Admirer."

Isabel stood there staring at the card. This was nothing like the other gifts she had received. The words were haunting. Sebastian grabbed the card to check for any other clues. He ripped open the box, pulled out the heart, looking to see if anything else was hidden inside.

"What were the other gifts you received?" he asked inquisitively. "Could anything be tied to the break in you had the other night?"

Izzy told him about the gift card, bouquet and photo of herself she'd received. She explained each gift and what was written on each card. Bash paced back and forth in the store endeavoring to put the puzzle pieces together. Fear crept up his spine as he contemplated the possibility of something happening to Izzy. While it might be an innocent crush, you couldn't leave anything up to chance. He would immediately report this to the police and ask them to be on the lookout for anyone or anything unusual, especially hanging out near the bookstore. Plus, in light of their recent conversation, Izzy might as well get use to the idea of him being around. He wasn't going anywhere any time soon.

Chapter 10

The day of the Arts & Crafts Festival had finally arrived. Tents lined the main street and roads were blocked off so visitors could freely roam tent to tent. As vendors unloaded their merchandise, Izzy could smell food being prepared on the grills that had been fired up for the day. The aroma made her mouth water. However, Izzy knew she must stay focused if she wanted to open on time. Pulling out the vintage lace she had purchased from a shop around the corner, she lined the tables with linen cloths then draped the antique lace, layering it top. Books, some wrapped in twine, were stacked in small groupings and laid in different areas on the decorated tables. She took old pearls and laid them around the vintage books, creating the perfect scene of days gone by. The look was finished with lace gloves and dried flowers. On one small table to the side, antique cups and saucers had been set up with a tea pot in the middle. A small sign read, "You can never get a cup of tea large enough or a book long enough to suit me, - C.S. Lewis." The booth screamed all things vintage, and Izzy was so proud she was able to create her vision.

The festival had just begun when Tristan strolled into Isabel's booth. "Good Morning," he said, acting a little standoffish.

"Hi there" answered Izzy. "I haven't seen you in quite a while. Where've you been hiding?"

"Oh, you know, just hanging around," replied Tristan. "I heard your apartment was burglarized. Everything okay?" His demeanor suggested he was a little concerned.

As far as Isabel knew, there were only a few people who knew about the break in. Of course, in a small town, you can't pee in a pot without someone else knowing about it and spreading a rumor. Izzy didn't get a chance to ask further questions because Tristan continued talking.

"I dropped by to see what kind of books you are trying to sell." Tristan began to look through the old books that Isabel had stacked on a makeshift bookcase.

While she was helping another customer, Bash wandered up to check out her booth. Although he might look like an interested customer, he had ulterior motives for checking in on Izzy.

"Well, if I had a nickel for every time you just showed up," came the sarcastic remark from Tristan, "I'd be rich at a penny arcade."

"I guess I could say the same for you," came Bash's response.

The guys squared up to one another and Isabel slid between them creating a neutral divide. She couldn't let two egomaniacs get after it right in the middle of all her hard work.

"I don't know what is going on with you two but pull it together. I'm trying to make money here and you're scaring my customers away," scolded Isabel. "Tristan thank you for stopping by and for your support. Sebastian, go get me something to drink." There was no mistaking the fact that both of them had been graciously dismissed.

By noon Isabel had sold everything in her booth. She couldn't have hoped for a more successful day. Letting down the sides of her tent, Izzy decided to close up shop. It was the perfect time to walk around and visit the other booths and vendors. Paintings, framed photographs, home décor, clothing, jewelry and anything else you could ask for lined the street. Izzy strolled from booth to booth, taking in all the sights and getting lost in the excitement of it all. She stopped at one booth and tried on a beautiful pair of earrings, chatting with the vendor.

Once the day had come to an end, Izzy packed up her belongings, took down her tent and tucked it all away inside the store. She was exhausted. A good hot bath and lounging in front of the TV sounded like the perfect plan.

"I think it's your turn to cook tonight," Bash said as she entered her own apartment.

"What is this 'turn' crap? This is my house. Mine, mine, *mine*. I walk in to find you relaxing on my sofa, eating my food, drinking my sweet tea...." Izzy was doing everything she could to keep from going ballistic.

"For the record, I bought several bags of groceries yesterday which included sweet tea."

"You're deliberately missing the point here," Izzy replied trying not to blow her top.

"I got the point. You don't like me being here and hovering. The point you're missing is I don't care." He smiled at her in spite of her mood. "I told Dottie I would watch after you and that's exactly what I'm going to do. So, go ahead, make your list, then we'll negotiate."

Isabel leered at him. He could be so infuriating at times.

"Rule number one," Iz perked up. "Whoever makes the meal or heats up the food, the other one cleans up. That's basic room-mate etiquette."

"Sounds good," Bash replied as he picked up his keys. "I need to run home and pick up a few things and will be back later." With that he leaned over to kiss her on top of the head.

"Rule number two, no kissing or physical contact," she nearly yelled as she realized that would keep things from get-ting confusing.

"Umm, no. I'm not going to agree to that one. Pick some-thing else."

"You said I get to make the rules," snapped Izzy.

"I also said we'd negotiate," smirked Bash.

"It makes things confusing," explained Izzy as if talking to a child.

"I'm not confused," His tone was equivalent to a shrug. "I know I want to be with you. I know how to go after what I want. It's about deciding."

"And what about what I want or what I decide?" questioned Isabel.

"You'll have to figure that out for yourself." Bash turned and looked at her to see her expression.

"I can't let you break my heart again," Izzy responded in almost a whisper.

"I never broke your heart," replied Bash.

"If you believe that, then what do we have to talk about? You seem to think you can just show up and everything picks up where you want it to for as long as you want it to?"

"Do you really want to know what I think? Are you ready to talk about it now?" asked Sebastian, waiting at the door for her response.

"No. I'm too tired to make any sense," answered Isabel. "Besides, it appears we don't have anything to talk about." With that she walked in the bathroom and shut the door. Isabel wasn't ready to relive the pain of their past. Not tonight.

Chapter 11

Time was flying by and Bayfront Books was starting to take shape. Isabel and Olivia's teamwork were starting to pay off. The store was looking good and beginning to make a profit. Ms. Dottie was stopping by today and Izzy wanted everything to look perfect. She was nervously dusting and putting away things, and it was obvious to Olivia she wanted to please the owner who had become like family.

"Good morning girls," came the cheery greeting as Dottie entered the store. This special lady was a breath of fresh air for Izzy. She loved her so much and hoped she would be pleased.

Just a few months earlier, Ms. Dottie had entered a rundown bookstore where the lack of attentiveness had been evident. It was now transformed into a warm, cozy and inviting piece of heaven. The walls were brushed in a warm khaki, the wooden bookcases looked polished like they'd been given a new chance on life. Stacks of book displays could be seen around the shop as well as a small reading corner set up in the back. Strawberry candles were lit, reminding everyone who entered that the

Strawberry Festival was just a few days away. Ms. Dottie wiped away a tear as she reached out to give each girl a big hug.

"I knew you were the right girl for the job, Isabel Porter," Ms. Dottie exclaimed as she continued to gaze around. "I am so incredibly proud of you."

"I just wanted to make you happy," Izzy replied. "You put a great deal of trust in me."

"I never doubted you for a second," raved Dottie. "Oh, by the way, it would seem I'm not the only one who has noticed you, Isabel." She produced a gift bag that she found in front of the door when entering.

Izzy stared at the package dreading to open it. The last gift proved to be a little strange with the broken heart inside. She was afraid of what she might find next.

"Aren't you going to open it?" asked Dottie, curious to know what was inside.

Isabel untied the ribbon and peered inside. She retrieved a little white box. Taking a deep breath, she opened the lid.

"Well, aren't those beautiful!" exclaimed Dottie.

"They look just like something you would pick out for yourself, Iz," remarked Olivia.

"They are something I would pick out for myself," whispered Isabel. "I tried these very earrings on at the Arts & Crafts Festival." Isabel cleared her throat and read the note aloud: "I had to buy these for you once I saw how much they complimented your beauty, Your Secret Admirer."

"You have a secret admirer?" asked Dottie with obvious excitement. "Oh my, how exciting."

"Or unsettling," murmured Izzy to Liv.

The bell rang on the front door announcing Tristan's arrival. Isabel admired how handsome he was, even if he were a bit odd at times. Tall, sandy brown hair, green eyes, and an athletic build. Any girl would be doing cartwheels to vie for his attention. Izzy was aware of his intentions towards her and wondered why she hadn't felt more flattered.

But of course, she knew why. For the past year she had deliberated over why she and Sebastian hadn't worked. They were friends first. Like every good relationship should start. Then over time their friendship had grown into love. How does one walk away from that so flippantly?

"So, what do you say?" asked Tristan again since Izzy hadn't answered him the first time.

"I'm sorry Tristan. My mind was wandering somewhere else. What did you ask me?"

"If you'd like to go to the Strawberry Festival with me on Saturday? Olivia said she could run things here. I'd love to introduce you to one of Loxley's finest events," explained Tristan.

Wanting to move forward regardless of her inhibitions, she

gladly agreed to go.

"Oh, and those earrings are beautiful," said Tristan before he left. "You should wear them on Saturday."

Lunch with Ms. Dottie was always fun and interesting. She had a sneaky way of bringing up the current state of Izzy's love life. In the year she lived with Ms. Dottie, they had spent many Saturday mornings over coffee, biscuits and sausage gravy talking about Isabel's frustration with Sebastian. Ms. Dottie had a way of bringing things into focus. Their love and concern for one another always managed to bridge the generational gap between them.

Once Izzy returned from lunch, she busied herself in the office the rest of the day. Being a good businesswoman was just as important as making a bookstore look pretty. Orders were placed, invoices were paid, and new books were arranged on the shelves. When exhaustion finally took over, Izzy locked up the store and took a walk to her favorite bench overlooking the bay. So much had happened since her arrival in Fairhope, at times it seemed like a lifetime ago.

She watched as Olivia met up with Chance along the bay walk. They made such a cute couple. Izzy closed her eyes and let the breeze off the water sweep across her face. She could smell the oaks and the green moss that hung low on the trees. The crash of the water against the pier was like a gentle massage soothing away her stress. The aura around the bay was so relaxing and always brought calm to her cluttered world.

"Are you relaxing or sleeping?" asked Bash, disrupting her peaceful moment.

"Well, if I were asleep, I'm not now." Izzy couldn't help but flash him a goofy grin.

"So, I was thinking today," continued Bash as he sat down beside her, "You've never been to the Strawberry Festival in Loxley. I wondered if you'd like me to show you around." Bash knew he couldn't propose it as a date, so he went the 'let me show you around' route.

Isabel never opened her eyes but casually responded, "I already have a date to the Strawberry Festival. Tristan asked if I'd like to go."

Sebastian felt like the wind had been knocked out of him. Thankfully her eyes remained closed, so she didn't see his embarrassment. When did Izzy start going on dates with Tristan? Bash had been with her every single moment except at work. How did Tristan swoop in and ask her out on a date?

"Oh, well good," replied Bash trying to sound as nonchalant as possible. "Glad you'll get to experience it."

Isabel opened one eye to see if Sebastian was being sincere. He didn't seem to mind at all. That was a relief, and a bit confusing. Maybe he didn't care for her as much as he'd tried to convince her he did. Perhaps it was time for them both to move on.

Quickly changing the subject, Bash commented on her earrings. "Those look really nice on you. They complement your eyes." He didn't wait around for a reply before leaving. The news of Izzy's date would more than occupy his mind for the remainder of the evening.

Chapter 12

"Explain to me again why you rented a tent at the Strawberry Festival?" asked Asher, looking at Sebastian confused.

"It's a good time to inform people there's a local marina nearby with affordable monthly rent." Bash busied himself stacking pamphlets hoping Asher couldn't read his face. "I also want to promote the "Rent-A-Boat Airbnb."

"I don't believe a word you just said," laughed Asher. "But I'm starting to get a much clearer picture." He nodded at two familiar faces who were approaching the tent. "Hi there Iz. Funny seeing you here."

Isabel shot a glance at Sebastian and looked around his tent. "So, you're advertising your marina at the Strawberry Festival?"

"Yep!" replied Bash staring directly into Izzy's eyes. "It's the perfect place to touch base with the locals".

"I don't believe I've met your *date,*" Asher interrupted staring down Tristan.

"Hi, I'm Tristan." He extended his hand to Asher but never glanced in Sebastian's direction. "I run the hardware store in

Fairhope. And now we should really get going because we have a full day and a great basket full of food."

Tristan placed his hand on Isabel's back purposefully guiding her away from the tent. If stares were daggers, Tristan would be dead. Asher stood silently observing the awkward exchange.

"As I said before, the picture is starting to become very clear," said Asher with a broad smile. "You are here to spy on Izzy and her Ken doll." Bash rolled his eyes and continued to look around trying to distract himself from the current events.

"Listen up bro, we've known each other for a long time so I'm going to give you a little advice from personal experience." Asher walked over and wrapped his arm around Bash's shoulder. "If you don't want to lose Izzy, you need to step up your game right now. Let her know you love her and want to marry her."

"Marry her?" Sebastian stuttered just saying the word. "Who said anything about marriage?"

"It's time Bash. Tell her how you feel." Asher gave him a brotherly punch in the arm then took off to meet all the single girls at the festival.

******

Izzy couldn't stop wondering: what in the Sam Hill did Sebastian think he was doing showing up at the Strawberry Festival running a tent? It was obvious to her he was only here to spy on her and Tristan. How was she supposed to concentrate on her date knowing he was over there, watching her?

"Does this look like a good spot to eat?" Tristan asked. "There's some shade here so we don't have to sit in the sun."

"Sure, this looks great," she replied and sat down on the blanket he spread out for them.

You could feel spring in the air. The weather hadn't turned hot or muggy just yet, and a day outside was just what she needed. Alabama was so lush and green in the spring. Azaleas bloomed and their fragrance floated on top of the breeze, filling the area with a sweet aroma. Laughter filled the air as friends greeted one another; kids played tag while waiting on mom to shop at a tent. You could smell the ripe strawberries that made your mouth water. Tristan promised to take her for the best strawberry shortcake at the festival once they finished eating their lunch.

"Tristan really was a nice guy," thought Izzy. He was kind and caring towards her. Treated her with respect. Everything she would expect from a true southern gentleman. Maybe if she gave it some time, he would eventually win her heart.

"I'm so glad you wore those earrings," stated Tristan. "I knew they would look good on you."

"What do you mean?" asked Izzy, confused at his comment.

"Oh, I mean...I just meant...." stammered Tristan, looking backed into a corner. "You know, when I saw you holding them at the store." Izzy was perplexed at his behavior but chalked it up to his odd personality at times.

Odd or not, Tristan treated her like a lady the whole day. They spent time visiting different tents and tasting samples of all things strawberry. He was right about the strawberry short-cake. It was divine. He even bought Izzy a jar of strawberry jam to take home as a souvenir. It turned out to be a very lovely day after all.

Once arriving back in Fairhope, Tristan walked Izzy to the back of the bookstore where a door led up to her apartment. She thanked him for a wonderful day and leaned up to give him a kiss on the cheek. Before her lips could reach his cheek, he blocked her attempt by turning his head and grazing his lips across hers. He pulled her close wrapping his arms tightly around her. As his grip intensified, Isabel managed to gently push away, allowing herself a respectable distance.

Waving goodbye, she made her way up the stairs to her apartment. Izzy thought long and hard about that kiss and what it might mean going forward. She wasn't sure how she felt about Tristan and didn't want to lead him on. Quietly opening the apartment door, she glanced over and saw Sebastian fast asleep on the sofa. Things could start to get really complicated.

Chapter 13

Izzy was enjoying the hot sun on her face and the breeze off the water as her toes dug down deep in the sand. She sat people watching and wrapped up in the glorious book she was reading. It was a beautiful day at the beach, and she didn't have a care in the world. But why was someone shouting her name? And what was that awful clanging she could hear?

"Isabel Porter, if you don't wake up right now," came the menacing sound of Sebastian's voice, "I'm bringing a glass of ice water and pouring it over your head!"

Izzy opened one eye and saw the clock read 5:00 a.m. "It's dark outside Bash. You better have a very good reason for waking me up!" barked Isabel. "And who is ringing that dadgum bell?"

"It's the Eastern Shore Jubilee," shouted Bash with little boy exuberance. "I'll explain on the way to the marina. Get dressed and make sure whatever you wear can get filthy and wet."

Isabel knew Sebastian Hadley very well and understood no amount of protesting would prevent him from bugging her until she was dressed. She appeared a few minutes later wearing tattered jeans, an old t-shirt and her hair pulled back in a ball cap. Izzy could hear the bells continuing to ring as they stepped outside. She begged Sebastian to explain what was going on as they made their way to the marina.

"A jubilee is a natural phenomenon that occurs sporadically on the shores of Mobile Bay," he began. "It's when an abundance of seafood washes up right at your feet." Sebastian was grinning from ear to ear and Izzy could tell he was extremely excited.

"Everyone in town will grab their buckets, fishing nets, water shoes, spears, spotlights, friends and family and make their way to the shores of the bay. It's fairly easy to fill several 5-gallon buckets full of shrimp. People will even fill up their pickup trucks with crabs or spear a hundred flounder. It just depends on what kind of species shows up. You've never seen anything like it, Iz."

By the time Bash finished explaining, they had arrived at the marina. He changed his clothes, put on some rubber boots and started grabbing buckets, fishing nets and a couple of fishing gigs. Isabel helped transport the gear trailing behind Bash as quickly as she could. When they reached the edge of the bay, people from town were everywhere. Moms, dads, kids and grandparents were in groupings along the shore. The word "jubilee" was the perfect description of this unusual event. Everyone was laughing and full of excitement. Bash instructed Izzy to grab a bucket and start scooping. He had grabbed an ice chest on his way out and as quickly as Izzy could scoop up shrimp, she was emptying them into the nearby ice chest. It was the most exciting fishing she had ever experienced.

"Look at me Bash!" squealed Isabel. She was muddy and wet and beaming. "This is like free food for months." It was at that moment Izzy looked down and saw a crab at her feet. She started hopping and dancing around trying to escape the bizarre creature. Losing the battle, she landed flat on her butt in the water and screamed as the crab inched its way towards her.

Sebastian was doubled over in laughter. Finally pulling himself together, he scooped Izzy up in his arms and away from the scandalous creature. For the first time since returning to Alabama, Izzy allowed herself to stare into Bash's eyes. The warmth they once shared was definitely still there. He sat her down away from the water but didn't remove his hands from her waist. Their old familiarity crept up surrounding them in a cloudlike aura. Izzy couldn't take her eyes off Sebastian's face. He pulled her close, leaned down and covered her mouth with his. Isabel didn't know if it was the morning air or the excitement of the jubilee, but she could feel his kiss to the tip of her toes. Sebastian finally pulled away, hoping he hadn't scared her away. Grabbing her hand, Bash ran back towards the bay hand-ing her a bucket with a wink.

A few hours later they were toting their haul back to the marina. Sebastian informed Izzy they needed to de-head the shrimp before they could be frozen. They spent hours on the dock cleaning all the seafood that was caught and tucked it away in Sebastian's freezer.

"I really had a great time, Bash," said Izzy. "Even if I had to wake up at the crack of dawn."

"You sound surprised," replied Sebastian. "We've always had a lot of fun."

"Fun was never our problem," smiled Izzy. "I'd be lying if I said I didn't enjoy your company. But there's so much more to a relationship than that Sebastian".

"So, you're saying you're still attracted to me, huh?" Sebastian broke out into a toothy grin and grabbed Isabel around the waist, pulling her close to nuzzle her neck.

Izzy laughed and wiggled away. "I need to go home and wash this fish smell off."

"I'll walk you back then I'm coming home to do the same," stated Sebastian.

"I'm a big girl," she smiled and gave him a flirty wink. "The sun is still up, and I'll be fine walking back to my apartment alone. Thanks for an already amazing day."

Watching her walk away with a big smile melted Sebastian's

heart. He anxiously awaited the day they would find their way back to one another.

Chapter 14

"What is that horrendous smell?" asked Izzy entering the bookstore for the first time that morning.

Olivia was at the register, holding her nose while trying to clean the counter and checking the trash for the atrocious odor. "I found this gift bag by the door this morning. I think the smell is coming from inside," said Olivia pushing the bag towards Isabel. "It's nauseating."

In an attempt to remove the revolting package as quickly as possible, Izzy untied the bag and peeked inside. She pulled out rotting flounder and shrimp in a zip lock bag. The card inside read, "You're the only fish in the sea for me, but you've killed my everlasting love for thee, Your Secret Admirer."

"What is wrong with this guy?" asked Liv holding her nose.

"What's wrong with what guy?" asked Bash as he bolted down from upstairs with coffee in hand.

"Izzy's secret admirer," answered Liv. "His gifts are growing creepier each time."

Sebastian headed towards the atrocious smell and peeked

inside the bag that sat on the counter. It nearly took his breath away. "What kind of secret admirer sends dead fish?" asked Bash.

"The kind who is trying to send me a message," mumbled Izzy. She took the card and handed it to Sebastian. He read the note with a twinge of anger flashing across his face.

"Maybe it's time I tell the police," suggested Isabel. "I recently noticed I had a nightgown missing from my dresser. I think it was taken during the break in. Maybe all these things have something to do with one another." Worry engulfed her face.

Sebastian looked relieved that she was finally putting the pieces together. Maybe now she would understand why his presence was needed at her place for the time being. There was some kind of psycho watching her every move and Sebastian had no intention of leaving her side.

"Tell you what, why don't you girls come to the marina tonight?" suggested Bash. "Chance and I will grill you up some great tasting seafood." He hoped it might take Izzy's mind off her stalker. This person may call himself an "admirer", but his behavior seemed more like a stalker. And that gave Sebastian reason to worry.

****

A few hours later the girls pulled up, right on time and could see smoke rising from a fire pit nearby. Bash definitely knew how to create ambience. Isabel used to tease him about his hidden talent. Looking around she could tell he had taken his gift and put it to good use. It was beautiful at the marina. Lights strung from tree to tree, twinkling in the night. The marina was well lit by the dock which allowed the lights to dance off the water. It was the perfect spot for friends to come and hang out.

Chance saw the girls right away and waved them over. Bash was seen stepping off a boat in the distance and headed over to welcome his guests. Their mouths began to water thinking of the scrumptious seafood that had been well prepared.

Izzy couldn't help but watch as Sebastian walked towards them. His tan skin and black hair looked great against his white shirt and khaki shorts. He had a way of carrying himself that assured those nearby that he was in charge. Her heart skipped a beat as those old familiar knots made a reappearance. If she wasn't careful, her vulnerability to those dark eyes and dashing smile could be fatal . Isabel didn't think she could survive her heart being broken by him again.

"Hi ladies," said Chance. "Glad ya'll could come hang out. Bash has been crafting his masterpiece all afternoon." He smiled at his boss with a big thumbs up.

"And what did you do?" asked Olivia, sending Chance a suspicious look. "Just here for moral support?"

"Well, someone has to be, right?" winked Chance coming over to sit next to Olivia.

Izzy watched the two love birds enjoying one another's company. Why did every other couple make it look so easy? Then she glanced at Bash as he was dishing up the food. Her heart ached for the way things had once been between them. They locked eyes when he handed her a plate of his tasty feast. Could he read in her eyes the confusion he caused her inside?

As the sun began its decent behind the horizon, orange and red hues formed a brilliant backdrop. Like hungry wolves, they devoured the wonderful seafood Sebastian had prepared with expert care.

As Olivia left to retrieve a bag from the car, Bash moved closer to Chance to give him a little piece of romance advice. "You look like you are smitten with Ms. Olivia my friend. Maybe it's time to go all in and commit. Get serious."

"And what exactly do you know about committing Mr. Hadley?" asked Isabel with a frown creasing her brow.

Sebastian shifted in his seat but was quickly saved as Olivia returned carrying the bag. Not missing a beat, he walked over to Izzy, hand extended and said, "Let's go. I'd like you to take an adventure with me."

"What are you talking about?" she glanced at Olivia to see what was happening.

"All I did was pack a few of your clothes," admitted Olivia, backing away with her hands up in a peaceful gesture, "as per requested." She shot Sebastian a knowing look then turned her attention to Chance. They quickly departed, hand in hand, happy to be alone for a while.

Chapter 15

"I know you enjoy a little adventure Iz. Will you please trust me?" asked Sebastian with total sincerity.

Izzy's mind was in a fog. Those four little words had haunted their relationship way before they ever became Isabel and Sebastian. But in spite of her doubts, she followed Bash to an exquisite cabin cruiser that was lit up and ready to depart. She had no idea if it was Sebastian's boat or if he was loaning it to himself, but the thrill of being on the water was always exhilarating.

The boat slowly eased out of the slip and headed into Mobile Bay. Izzy and Bash glanced back and waved at Olivia and Chance standing on the dock. They were obviously smitten with one another and Chance took the opportunity of being left alone by slipping his arm around Olivia's waist.

"Looks like they are happy to see us go," said Izzy in a sly voice.

"Well, I left Chance the keys to the marina and the upstairs porch! Looks like the boy is taking my advice."

"Lord I hope not. Besides, I don't think Liv is that kind of girl," offered Izzy.

"You don't think any girl is that kind of girl…except Emma." Isabel slapped Sebastian on the shoulder and he laughed out loud as he eased down on the throttle and the boat began to glide through the slick water.

"I'm going down below and take a look around," announced Izzy.

"Go ahead. But if you're looking for Tristan," Sebastian replied, trying not to sound jealous. "He's not down there."

Izzy wasn't amused. "If that's what this trip is going to be about you can turn this boat around right now mister!"

"Easy darlin'. I was only implying that every time we're alone, he shows up".

"That's funny. He says the same thing about you." Izzy felt a tinge of satisfaction seeing Bash go quiet because he knew it was true.

"Okay, okay. How bout' a truce, Iz?" begged Sebastian. "I wanted to be alone with you, where we had no distractions. A little time for us to be together and maybe talk like old times".

Izzy's mind was rolling like the small swells in the bay. What she thought was going to be an evening at the marina had now turned into an overnight trip with Sebastian. She wondered what his intentions were going to be as the evening progressed.

Climbing into the captain's chair next to Bash, she laid her head back against the seat and let the cool, night air blanket her face. It didn't take long before they fell into their old routine. Bash pointing out areas of interest and Isabel listening intently to his stories. She was always amazed that this guy she thought of as a player in school was so interested in the history and life of what he called "God's Country." As they passed several natural gas rigs, Bash told Izzy they provided jobs, income and resources for the state, but he hated how they took away from the scenery of the bay. Isabel always enjoyed him talking about his home state. His passion was undeniable.

"Are you bored yet?" asked Bash looking over to see if Izzy had fallen asleep.

"Of course not. You can tell a good story better than anyone I know."

"Okay good, cause I've got one more," he said with a grin. "Fort Morgan and Fort Gaines, which are on Dauphin Island, defended Mobile from enemy ships trying to enter the bay. Just imagine the Civil War, when the Union ships were stationed just outside the entrance to the bay. The forts stood strong defending their territory. Confederate blockade runners would try to slip past the ships and into the bay delivering much needed supplies. It was a great game of cat and mouse."

"Well, no one knows a game of cat and mouse better than you," teased Izzy.

Bash rolled his eyes at the jab as he turned the boat east towards Destin. He stayed close enough to the coast for Izzy to enjoy the lights on the shore. He knew being out on the water always put her in a good mood. A perfect set up for a much-needed conversation.

The boat suddenly slowed and Bash looked worried as he tapped on the fuel gauge. Izzy instantly became alert. While she loved being on the water, the thought of getting stuck out in the vast darkness was eerie.

"I think we're out of gas," Bash yelled as he ran below to check the tanks.

"How could he be so stupid?" Izzy's heart was beating fast and furious. It was a mixture of fear and anger. "Who starts on a boat ride, at night, in the Gulf of Mexico and doesn't check the fuel?" she barked.

"Well, there's some good news and some bad news," confirmed Sebastian as he returned from below. "The bad news is we are out of fuel. When my renter asked if I could bring his boat down to Destin for him, it never dawned on me to check if there was gas in the tank," explained Sebastian. "But don't worry. I called a friend who's bringing us some fuel from the marina right away. It should be enough to get us to Orange Beach, which is where you see those lights right there." Bash put an arm around her shoulder and pointed out the lights to assure

Izzy they weren't far away from shore.

She stared at him. Being stuck on the ocean at night was not her idea of relaxing. Why did things like this always happen with Sebastian?

"The other good news is I thought ahead and brought us some wine and snacks. I'll open the wine for you, but I better drink a Coke in case the marine police decide to check us out."

"You remembered wine and snacks but forgot to check if there was fuel in the boat?" Izzy was practically yelling. "Mr. boy scout, always prepared, forgets to check the gas in the boat?"

"But I remembered the snacks. Don't I get a little credit for that?" he asked batting his eyes and trying to look cute.

Isabel's eyes shot daggers at him. She turned her back while Sebastian dropped anchor. He left on the running lights which created a strange calmness to the whole scene. Under any other circumstances she may have enjoyed the inviting atmosphere.

Wanting to keep her wits about her, she asked Sebastian for a soda. He gave her a quizzical look because all southerners call any kind of soda a Coke. He continued unpacking the bag and pulled out a small container of little chicken salad sandwiches, cheese straws, and homemade cookies. She was impressed.

"I have to say, I'm a little shocked. This looks just like the food Ms. Dottie had at the street party." Even in the dim light, she could see the sheepish grin on Bash's face.

"These are Ms. Dottie's!" He laughed.

"What? How?" asked Izzy. "Does she know about this little adventure of yours tonight?"

"I may have let it slip the other day when I talked to her," admitted Bash.

"And she just offered to cater your little rendezvous?" Izzy's voice was becoming louder by the minute. "Wait…you told her we were going on an overnight trip together on a boat?"

"Relax Iz. Ms. Dottie knows you and all about your virtue. She didn't think a thing about it. She was thrilled when I asked if she would fix us a meal".

Isabel was furious with the whole situation. She now could add embarrassment to her list of grumblings about this unexpected trip. She glanced over and took a peek at Ms. Dottie's food. It looked delectable and did bring a sense of comfort, so she reluctantly took a sandwich hoping to calm her nerves.

Bash sat next to her hoping to regain some of the footing he lost with the empty fuel tank. "Do you remember how small of a beach town Gulf Shores was when we were growing up?" He glanced over at Isabel to see if she was softening up a little bit. "Before Hurricane Frederic there were only a few shops and restaurants, the little amusement park on the corner and the putt-putt golf place. It was mostly a private beach with cabins."

Izzy was lost in thought remembering how it use to be. "I remember the Pink Pony Pub and watching it get washed away with one giant wave. I don't think I'll ever forget how Hurricane Frederic changed so many things around here."

"You got that right. Heck, Orange Beach wasn't even a town. Just an undisturbed beach. Now it's a huge resort area with condos lining the beach and tons of restaurants and entertainment. People come from all over to visit."

Izzy stared at the lights sparkling on shore and realized what he said was true. She remembered lazy days at the beach when teenagers would cruise past The Hangout and girls would bake in the tropic sun. Boys spent a lot of time trying to impress the girls which typically meant getting into trouble. Isabel remembered stories of Bash and his posse but never knew how many were actually true.

"So, I was thinking," Bash began, making Isabel tense. "You know I tend to overthink things, right?"

"Well, you didn't overthink putting fuel in the boat, did ya'?" Izzy couldn't help but smirk.

"Come on Iz, I'm trying to be serious." She could see he was searching for just the right words, which meant he was trying to say something important. He stood up so he could expend some of his nervous energy. "I have thought and thought about what happened between us. I assumed that things were going along great. The distance was hard, but we were making it work." He paused to see Isabel's reaction then continued. "Then you got busy with work and we missed a few visits." Noticing Isabel's furrowing brow, Bash tried to retrace his steps, not aiming to put the blame on her.

"I know I couldn't come down a few times, but never once did I blame you when you couldn't come to visit me," snapped Izzy, becoming very defensive.

"I know you didn't. But then I started thinking maybe I was holding you back. You've never been a person to stay put. You love to travel, see the world and live in new places. I'm just a home boy. I've never lived more than an hour away in any direction." Sebastian's face was etched in frustration with himself and his choices.

"I don't know where you came up with this kind of thinking," said Izzy. She was frustrated too but wasn't entirely sure why.

"I thought about the first time I saw you at the coffee shop. There you were, a hot shot reporter from the city, doing a story about the Deep South," Bash sat back down to look Isabel directly in the eye. "And I suddenly realized "I" was the Deep South." They sat quietly as that thought sank in. "I never expected anything to happen between us and I'm not sorry it did. But I didn't want you to wake up one day feeling like you missed out on what you wanted to do with your life."

Izzy sat quietly staring at him. He was not looking at her but alternating between looking at the bottom of the boat and out into the ocean. She knew he was serious, which for this man was a rare emotion.

"Bash, I never said I was unhappy," replied Isabel. "Yes, I love to travel and see new things. I wanted to do that with you." She sat quietly, staring at the top of his head, until he finally looked up. "I know you are as rooted here as the big oaks on the bay. But there is a whole world out there to see. You could have always come back home".

"Can you Iz? Do you think you could ever come back home"?

A flurry of questions raced through Isabel's head: What was he asking? Was he asking her to come back to Alabama? Was he asking her to give them another chance?

Sebastian continued. "I've never been a big fish here at home, but when I was around your publisher friends I felt like the smallest fish in a big pond."

Izzy was speechless. Bash never had a problem intermingling with people around Mobile. It didn't matter if they were wealthy professionals or the dock hands at the marina. He was always the same. If Sebastian was uncomfortable at her work parties, it never showed.

"Maybe it's just pride. Maybe I'm trying to make excuses,"

he admitted. "It's about me and my feeling uncomfortable. You never gave me a reason to feel less of a person."

"And I never asked you to move to the city. This is why you broke it off with me?" asked Izzy trying to gather what thoughts she had left. "What about talking things out, Bash? What about communicating how you feel and what you're thinking?" Isabel was growing heated just thinking about everything she had gone through over the past year. She stood up so she could pace.

"I didn't want to hold you back, so I cut it off," snapped Sebastian showing his frustration.

"So, you made the decision for both of us. What am I supposed to do with that? Just act like it will never happen again and pick up where we left off?"

"I never stopped loving you Iz," Sebastian spoke in a hushed voice, as if that very confession tore open his heart.

How was this considered love? She had been in torment for over a year wondering what she had done to push him away. Isabel gazed out at the water taking the time to steady her emotions. Bash made his way to stand directly behind her and gently placed his hands on her waist. Isabel tensed at his touch. He softly whispered just loud enough for her to hear. "I am so sorry for hurting you Iz. That was never my intention. Can you try to forgive me? I really need for you to forgive me."

Isabel slowly turned to face him while Bash kept his hands

securely at her waist. "I can always forgive you Bash," she never took her eyes from his. "I just don't know if I can ever trust you again."

Sebastian stared into those beautiful brown eyes that had captivated him since the day they ran into each other at the coffee shop. He could see the hurt written all over her face and knew one night on a boat wasn't going to solve all that had transpired between them. He leaned down and gently kissed her. To his surprise, Izzy didn't pull away. Her lips parted and he pulled her even closer, kissing her again with a fervor. When they parted, Isabel stepped back hoping Sebastian couldn't feel her racing heart.

The waves made the boat roll to one side and they both lost their balance. "I knew I still made you weak in the knees," Sebastian said in his most southern accent.

Isabel shot him a look that said, "In your dreams buddy boy." She shivered a little, unaware if it was from the kiss or how cool it can get at night, even during an Alabama summer.

When Sebastian returned from getting her a blanket, Isabel asked how long it would take for his friend to arrive. With a sly smile and wink he climbed into the captain's chair, flipped a switch, and when he turned the key the big inboard engine roared to life.

"What in the world..." She looked at Bash in utter astonishment. "Did you just lie about the whole thing?"

Bash reached over and squeezed her hand. "I didn't lie about still loving you."

Izzy knew he meant it, at least for the moment. But it would take more than one night to change her mind. That kiss, however, would burn in her memory long after tonight faded away.

****

As the lights of Pensacola came into view, Bash decided to break the silence by telling more of his stories. "We used to stay in Pensacola when I was little. There's a famous Irish pub here called McGuire's. They have a great St. Paddy's Day party. It starts with a run where people are dressed in crazy costumes and at the end of the race they serve green beer and Irish punch." Sebastian looked over to see if Izzy was listening. She sat quiet and still, looking out towards the city, taking it all in. He wished he knew what she was thinking, about him and all he had shared.

He continued, "I don't know if you knew this, but Pensacola is the home of the Blue Angels. It is quite a sight to see. I'd love to share that with you some time."

Sebastian couldn't help but glance at Isabel sitting in the moonlight. She was quiet but seemed to be enjoying the peaceful ride. It was after midnight when Sebastian pulled the boat into the slip at the Destin marina. He was thankful for calm seas and no wind. The last thing he wanted was to put a mark on the owner's boat. A security guard was making his rounds and helped with the mooring lines before going on his away again.

Izzy had enjoyed the ride, but it had been a long day. "I hope where we're staying isn't too far away. I'm beat." She was physically and emotionally drained.

"Well, you're in luck," he came over and turned Izzy towards the area below. "You have arrived at your night accommodations."

Izzy turned around in surprise. "We are spending the night on the boat?" She asked excitedly. The waves rocking the vessel back and forth and the riggings on the sailboats slapping the masts ought to put her right to sleep. "I'm so excited I'm going down to get ready for bed."

"Oh yeah, Iz...don't spend too much time looking for pajamas. I told Olivia that you wouldn't be needing them!" Sebastian said chuckling to himself.

"What is wrong with you? What will she think? She already suspects something is up with you sleeping at my apartment. I swear I could kill you!" Izzy stomped down the steps and Sebastian could hear her practically tearing the overnight bag apart. A few minutes later she emerged wearing a pair of long pajama pants and a shirt.

"You do like to get your jollies, don't you?"

"I guess Olivia knows you better than I do," Bash grinned. He walked over and softly kissed her on the forehead. "Promise me you'll consider what we talked about tonight?"

"I'll think about it, but I can't promise I'll change my mind," replied Izzy. "Where are you going to sleep?"

"I never got to have my wine. I think I'll play a little Jimmy Buffet music and have a glass or two." Sebastian watched as Isabel slipped beneath the deck below. She had no idea how much she affected him. His mind was cluttered from their earlier conversation. He hoped somehow, someway, she had heard his heart. As he laid there, looking up into the dark of night, his mind raced back to that unexpected kiss they shared under the moon. There are some things you never want to forget.

Chapter 16

"A tropical system needs three things to develop: warm water, high moisture, and low wind shear. This system usually has sustained winds ranging between 39 and 73 miles per hour. It's characterized by a low-pressure center and by several thunderstorms that create strong winds and heavy rain. As these storms travel, the wind, rain, and storm surge destroy the shoreline, villages, and cities in their path."

Izzy turned off the TV. She had been listening intently to the weather station nearly 24/7. The talk of this tropical storm headed for the southern coast made her uneasy. She remembered all too well living through Hurricane Frederic. The eye of the hurricane passed right over Mobile where she was living. The aftermath was devastating. The neighborhoods looked like bombs were dropped snapping trees in half like broken matchsticks. Cars were tossed three blocks from home. Houses were destroyed. Gulf Shores completely disappeared. The memory of that experience haunted her now as a dangerous, tropical storm was likely headed their way.

Isabel had walked down to Camille's for coffee and was making her way slowly back to the bookstore. She saw shop owners with plywood leaned against the sides of their shops waiting to be boarded across the windows if necessary.

Main Street was typically a cheery place to stroll down in the mornings. You could feel more tension in the air today, as if people were bracing for the inevitable. As Izzy neared the shop door, she saw a gift bag sitting out front. It had been a while since she'd heard from her secret admirer. The absence of gifts had provided much needed stress relief. Now it was back and staring her in the face. She picked up the bag, unlocked the door and headed straight for the counter. The anticipation was just as bad as the actual gift.

Izzy quickly untied the bag and reached inside. It was heavier than the other gifts, and as she pulled it out, she could see it was definitely shiny.

"Is that a really big flashlight?" asked Liv as she entered the store. "I guess he's going for practical now?"

Isabel read the card aloud, "For when you find yourself in the dark, Your Secret Admirer."

This guy was creeping her out, and she wanted to make sure the police were aware of this latest gift. She told Olivia she was going to her office to give them a call and disappeared into the back of the store. In the background she could hear the bell ringing, indicating customers were arriving for the day.

"Okay so I've made you a list because I know how much you like lists and checking things off." Sebastian came charging into her office, never stopping to take a breath. "First, know your evacuation routes and maybe even write it down. Second, you need a home safety kit. Third, have a place to go for safety. Fourth..."

"Whoa Bessy...what in the world are you talking about?" Izzy tried to interrupt to no avail.

"Make sure and get some cash out and fill up your gas tank and your generator."

"I don't have a generator," answered Isabel blankly.

Sebastian was nervously pacing and appeared very anxious. He knew he'd be asked to go out with the Coast Guard Auxiliary with the storm coming in so quickly. He didn't want to leave Isabel alone to weather the storm. There was no one he cared for more than her, but he felt compelled to help out any way he could getting people to safety.

"So, this is what we're going to do," stated Sebastian not asking for Izzy's input. "I want you to come to my place when the weather picks up. I'll have Chance, Olivia and Asher come too so you aren't there alone."

Isabel got up, guided Bash to her chair and firmly sat him down. "You need to tell me what you're talking about and why you're acting like a lunatic."

"The storm is rolling in fast Iz, and I'm worried about you," Sebastian explained. "But I'm part of this Coast Guard Auxiliary, so it's my job to help out the Coast Guard, especially during tropical storms. I will be away part of the time tonight as the storm picks up, but I want you to be with people and not alone. I have to know you're with someone or I won't go." Sebastian's eyes were pleading. She could tell he needed her reassurance. "I also brought plywood with me and left it outside. Asher is coming by later to hang it on the store windows for you."

"Okay Bash. As soon as the weather starts getting bad, I'll head to the marina and meet you there."

"Please…please go to the marina and I'll be back as soon as I can." Bash kissed her on the cheek and left her office looking worried.

****

Business had been slow at the bookstore all day. A few customers had stopped in and were buying books to read while riding out the storm. In preparation of the coming storm, Izzy decided to close early and sent Olivia home. The banging outside caught her attention and she walked to the front to see if Asher had arrived. He was outside working up a sweat securing the boards to the window.

"I never thought in a million years you would be doing something nice for me this many years later," smiled Izzy. When they broke up during their high school years, she didn't think her and Asher could ever be friends again. Now here he was boarding up the windows to Ms. Dottie's bookstore for her. They chatted for a few minutes as the wind began picking up. Excusing herself to finish up a few more things, she told Asher she'd meet the rest of them at the marina shortly.

Once back inside the bookstore, Izzy couldn't believe how dark it was with the windows boarded up. She hurried back to the office to finish looking over a few bills she felt couldn't wait.

Once or twice Isabel glanced out the window to see the wind whipping trees around and the band of rain that soon followed. How long she had been working she wasn't sure when the lights began to flicker in the office. Isabel knew she had a tendency to get caught up in her work and lose track of time, and when she glanced over at the clock it had been an hour. The lights flickered one more time before they finally went out.

Izzy grabbed the flashlight her secret admirer had given her and ran up the stairs to her apartment. It may have been a creepy gift, but right now it would come in handy. She wanted to grab a few clothes in case she got soaked on her way over to the marina. When the knocked sounded on her apartment door, her heart jumped into her throat. She stood shocked and frozen.

"Hey Izzy, its Tristan," came the voice on the other side of the door.

"Dear lord, Tristan, you scared me to death," said Izzy as she opened the door. "What in the world are you doing here?"

"I thought you might need some extra water," he replied as he carried bags of groceries to her kitchen counter. "I picked up some canned food and a few other items that will last in case we are without power for a few days."

Suddenly standing in her apartment with the lights out, Tristan's foreboding presence made Izzy more on edge than re-assured. As he began to put the weeks' worth of groceries away, Tristan's presumed ownership of the place began to fill her with uneasiness. He was talking to her about the storm, where she should hide if things became dangerous, but Izzy wasn't listening. She was trying to think of the best way to tell Tristan she was expected at the marina. He walked over and picked up the flashlight she had laid on the end table.

"Wow, great flashlight, Iz," said Tristan. "This is one of those heavy-duty kinds that you need for storms just like this."

"It was a gift," mumbled Izzy. "And I'm really going to need it when I head over to the marina."

Tristan's jaw tightened with the latest revelation. She could tell he was trying to measure his words.

"Look Izzy," replied Tristan with as much control as he could muster. "I can't let you do that."

Isabel's heart rate quickened. She had no idea what was going on in his mind, but he couldn't hold her hostage in her own apartment. She was going through scenarios in her mind when Tristan interrupted.

"It's way too dangerous to be out in this weather," he stated in a cool tone. "That's why I came here. To take care...to help you."

As long as Isabel kept her wits about her, she really didn't think he would hurt her. Tristan said he came to help her. Maybe he had a weird way of expressing his concern. She decided to go over and make herself something to eat. Keeping things as normal as possible seemed like the best idea under the circumstances.

"You know I told Bash and Asher I would head to the marina when the weather started getting bad," Isabel said as calmly as possible. "They're expecting me."

"I'm sure Sebastian will get over it," came the biting response. "I've had to learn to share myself. Besides, it's too dangerous for you to be out there by yourself."

What in the world was he talking about? Isabel was beginning to think Tristan wasn't as stable as he had always seemed. He wasn't acting like himself and it was making her nervous. She sat at the little dinette table in the kitchen trying to appear normal and eating the sandwich she had made for herself. The wind was howling, and the rain was beating against the windows. The tension in the room could be cut with a knife.

"Isabel Porter what are you doing?" shouted Bash as he rushed into the apartment. "I went to the marina first and found out you hadn't been there."

Izzy jumped to her feet and met Sebastian halfway across the room. She grabbed his hand and he could feel her shaking. It didn't take him long to survey the room and see Tristan standing in the kitchen holding a knife. Before he got the wrong idea, Izzy blocked his path to explain the current situation.

"Hey Bash, sorry," quivered Izzy's voice. "I worked longer than I had planned to, lost electricity and when I was packing a few things, Tristan showed up with water and groceries." Isabel's eyes were very expressive as if trying to communicate something more than what her words were saying. Sebastian stopped mid-stride trying to read between the lines. He knew Izzy well enough to know she wasn't comfortable with the situation at hand.

"Sebastian, I have been taking care of Isabel," stated Tristan.

"She's in good hands and you can take yourself back to where you came from."

Before Bash responded with more than just words, Isabel intervened. "Listen Tristan. I did promise Sebastian and Asher earlier today that I would spend the evening with them." She had no idea how he would take this but there was no way she was letting Bash leave without her.

If looks could kill, Bash and Izzy would be dead. Tristan stood his ground as if he had no intention of throwing in the towel. Isabel went over to her bag, zipped it up and joined Sebastian by the door.

"Come on Tristan. I have to lock up everything before I can go."

Reluctantly, he followed them down the stairs and out the door. He didn't say a word once they were outside but simply ran away looking for shelter. Bash and Izzy ran to his car and once inside Izzy broke down crying, releasing the pent-up emotion that had built over the past hour.

Chapter 17

The drive to the marina was harrowing, quiet and eerie. Neither Bash nor Izzy spoke. Both were trying to digest the scene that had taken place in her apartment. Sebastian was trying to concentrate on the road and the terrible driving conditions. His mind kept wavering between anger at Tristan and concern for Izzy. She was just staring ahead, looking but not seeing. The only noise was the wind, the pounding rain and the roar of the truck engine.

It was dark and the headlights reflected off the slanting rain that looked like a sheet of water. The trees waved back and forth in the wind. Occasionally a limb or piece of debris blew across the road.

"Watch out!" screamed Izzy. Sebastian slammed on the brakes and the truck skidded to a halt. A few more inches and he would have hit a big tree limb laying in the road. The truck lights shining on the leaves hid the limb making it blend in with the blowing rain. Izzy was frantic. She was embarrassed for yelling out, but her nerves were frazzled. Bash was mad and ashamed. He had been focused on the road but had taken a quick glimpse over at Iz to see how she was doing. He was on top of the limb before he knew it and was very thankful she had seen it. They both took a deep breath and looked at each other.

"It's just a big limb," replied Sebastian. "I think I can get around it, then the marina is just at the bottom of the hill. We need to get there as soon as we can."

Izzy nodded and watched as Bash eased the truck off the shoulder of the road and around the limb. The branches scraped the sides of the truck and Sebastian cringed just a little. He was particular about his truck, but this wasn't the time to dwell on such things. Once around the limb, he pulled back on the road and headed for the marina, this time keeping his eyes on the road.

Bash and Izzy were soaking wet by the time they entered his apartment. Asher had fired up the generator when they lost power and him, Chance and Olivia were gathered around the TV watching the latest report about the approaching tropical storm. It was obvious to the group Isabel had been crying and they all rushed over to see if she was hurt.

"Where have you been?" asked Asher. "We got worried when you didn't show up after a couple of hours."

"I'll fill you guys in later," answered Sebastian. "I think we're both hungry and want to get changed out of these wet clothes."

Bash kept his arm around Izzy and led her into his bedroom. He suggested she go into his bathroom and change, and he would change out in the room. After dressing, she opened the bathroom door and saw Sebastian had changed into a cyan blue t-shirt with faded jeans. His hair was still damp as he sat on the edge of the bed waiting for her.

"Do you feel like talking about it yet?" He was searching her eyes to see if she was any steadier. "You were shaking so bad when you grabbed my hand in your apartment the only thing I wanted to do was get you out of there as fast as I could before I did something that landed me in jail."

"I don't know what to think," murmured Isabel. "Tristan didn't do anything to me but from the moment he showed up, I had an eerie feeling. It only became worse the longer he was there."

"I don't know what he would have done with that knife had you not stepped between us," replied Sebastian. "He had a peculiar look in his eye."

Isabel walked over, sat on the bed and squeezed Sebastian's hand. "I can't thank you enough for coming to look for me." Tears welled up in her eyes and she quickly brushed them away. As another tear escaped, Bash reached up and gently wiped it away letting his hand linger on her cheek.

"I will always come looking for you," replied Bash. "I let you go once. I won't let that happen again." He lovingly wrapped his arms around Izzy. She didn't resist. The warmth of his embrace was soothing and for the first time in a long time she just wanted to feel comforted.

"Hey guys," yelled Asher. "We made some sandwiches out here."

As they joined the others in the living area, Izzy spotted Emma for the first time. She had no idea Emma was going to be here tonight. How had Bash left that little tidbit out of their earlier conversation? Isabel wondered if she would ever be comfortable when Emma was around? As a teen she had begun to realize that insecurity was something you had to repair yourself. It's not someone else's fault. Emma had been part of Bash's life since high school. They had dated back then and eventually decided to just be friends. However, Izzy felt Emma still carried a torch for Bash. She didn't know how to handle the situation.

"It looks like the storm could be turning," stated Sebastian listening intently to the newscast. "But they won't know for sure until the middle of the night. I think everyone should plan on bunking down here for the evening."

"Good thing because I had already planned on it," purred Emma smiling. "Hey, let's get a group pic to post on Instagram. My phone is blowing up from people out-of-state checking on us. We can post our little hurricane party!"

Izzy was in no mood for festivities, but she didn't want to make a scene. She was doing her best to overcome her insecurities about Emma. However, when the group gathered in front of the bar, Isabel made sure to squeeze in close to Bash. Olivia was practically draped over Chance. That left Asher and Emma as an obligatory couple, at least for the photo.

Olivia and Chance brought the sandwiches and chips over to the table. Everyone gathered around and enjoyed the food they had prepared. The TV blared in the background as the weathermen continued to guess which path the storm would take. Earlier in the day the forecast models had all aligned and showed the storm making landfall around Mobile Bay. Updated models now showed the storm was moving more towards the West. The colored lines showed the different projected paths and looked like spaghetti on the TV screen.

The wind could be heard whipping the boats in the marina and the rain was pelting the windows so hard it sounded like hail. Sebastian explained the marina owned a big forklift and most of the smaller boats had been lifted into dry storage and put in the warehouse behind the marina. The boat owners with trailers had already pulled their boats from the water and taken them to a safer area. The larger boats were the only ones to remain. Bash, Chance and Asher had spent the morning double lashing them to the floating piers. Sebastian prayed the new design would save the boats and his little marina.

Isabel walked to the area of the apartment Bash called the porch where he had a big bed swing hung to one side. There was a wall of windows overlooking the marina that could be unlocked, slid open and looked similar to a balcony. There hadn't been time to board the windows. It was hard to see through the glass because of the driving rain. Izzy marveled at the strength of the winds and the angry waves crashing against the dock. She felt oddly afraid and curious at the same time.

Comfortable chairs were set up on the other side of the porch creating a cozy little sitting area. Isabel wandered over to the bed swing and laid down. She found a blanket nearby and covered up. She really wasn't in the mood for a crowd and the emotion of the evening had been exhausting. She could hear the others laughing and talking as she closed her eyes for just a few minutes.

****

Izzy woke up in a panic when she heard heavy breathing next to her ear. She thought it was a nightmare until she looked over her shoulder and saw Bash asleep next to her. For a moment she could see Tristan's face. She remembered that scary hollow look in his eyes as she ushered him out of her apartment the evening before.

She glanced around the two rooms where bodies were strewn everywhere, wrapped up in blankets and sleeping bags. The TV was still on and with just a glance Izzy could see the worst of the storm had sidestepped them. While they had received high winds and lots of rain, the damage would be minimal. Izzy meandered to the windows looking out over the marina. She stared into the dark. Occasionally during a break in the clouds, the moon would cast an eerie light on the bay.

Bash moved and his heart quickened when he didn't feel Isabel lying next to him. The sheets were damp and tangled from a fitful sleep, but he definitely recognized the scent of Izzy's perfume. It took him a moment to remember the storm and the events at the bookstore earlier that evening.

He glanced around the room until he spotted a lovely silhouette standing by the windows. His heart quickened at the site of Isabel in the night. Bash sat up and admired her from a distance. This was not how he pictured it would be when Isabel came over to his place for the first time. He wanted a candle lit dinner on the porch overlooking the marina as the moon reflected off the water. He wanted to be alone. And yet now, he had a room full of people sleeping everywhere. It was far from perfect. How could one lady cause so much peace and so much havoc inside of him?

Sebastian quietly got up, hoping not to wake the others. He moved behind Isabel and placed his arms around her waist.

"You are a sight for sore eyes," he whispered into her ear. "I got worried when I didn't feel you next to me."

"I was just staring out at the bay and wondering how it could be causing so much havoc one minute and be peaceful the next?" She stood in silence as if mesmerized.

Sebastian pulled her close until her head rested against his shoulder. "I know exactly what you mean."

Chapter 18

Weeks had passed and the whole town of Fairhope was still cleaning up debris from the tropical storm that had passed through. Izzy and Liv had removed the wood from the windows and picked up debris outside that had blown around during the storm. Neighbors were helping neighbors; everyone had been busy trying to put the town back together.

While shelving books at the store one morning, Isabel saw Tristan passing by the front windows and dashed to the back of the store to avoid contact. She hadn't spoken to him since the night of the storm. She still felt anxious every time she thought of that night.

"Hi Olivia," said Tristan as he entered the store. "I was wondering if Izzy is around?"

Olivia was just starting to respond when Izzy appeared from the back of the store. She looked right past Tristan and proceeded to ask Olivia a question.

"Have you seen a book titled 'Don't Fear'?" asked Izzy. "I'm worried I might have sold it at the Spring Festival on accident. It was a special vintage book I found in one of the packed boxes."

Olivia looked around the counter and in some books on hold for customers but couldn't find anything.

"I'll keep an eye out for sure," replied Liv.

Izzy started towards the back of the store again when Tristan intercepted her mid-stride.

"Can I talk to you for a second, Isabel?" asked Tristan. "I've meant to come by sooner, but the hardware store needed some repair after the storm."

"I'm kind of busy today," she answered, hoping he wouldn't pursue further conversation.

"I wanted to apologize for showing up at your apartment the night of the storm," explained Tristan. "I only wanted to check on you and make sure you were okay. I left wondering if I had scared you instead. You seemed a little uneasy when Sebastian showed up."

Isabel wasn't sure how to respond. He seemed sincere in his apology, and maybe it was just a misunderstanding on her part.

"It's fine Tristan. I think I was already a little spooked to begin with and then when you showed up unexpectantly, right after the power went out, it unnerved me a little."

"I felt I might have upset you," explained Tristan, "and that's the last thing I ever wanted to do. I hope you can forgive me and we can still be friends." He looked at her with puppy dog eyes and a sincere smile.

"Of course we are friends," said Izzy. "Don't think any more about it." She ushered Tristan to the front door assuring him all was fine between them. As he was leaving, Ms. Dottie came bounding through the entrance.

"What a pleasant surprise," exclaimed Isabel as she reached out and gave the older lady a heartfelt hug. "To what do we owe the honor of your presence Ms. Dottie?"

"Hush now girl," replied Dottie with a light chuckle. "I wanted to stop by and check on the store for one thing. And second, I wanted to ask you girls about attending the Grand Summer Ball."

Olivia squealed in delight, causing Izzy to nearly jump out of her skin. She had no idea why Liv was so giddy about the unexpected invitation.

"It's the event of Fairhope Izzy," exclaimed Olivia. "It's for the high society people." She was grinning from ear to ear and excitedly jumping up and down.

"I don't know about high society people," laughed Ms. Dottie with a slight blush. "But it's for a good cause and I've bought a table for the event. I would like you two young ladies to be my guests."

"Well, I think you already know Olivia's response," smiled Isabel. "And I'd love to come to anything you invite me to Ms.

Dottie." She gave the older lady another hug, showing her just how much she appreciated her and the invitation.

Before Dottie left, the girls had made plans to get their hair and nails done together in Fairhope and Ms. Dottie would get dressed at Izzy's. They could hardly wait for the evening of the grand event.

Chapter 19

Isabel and Olivia walked proudly behind Ms. Dottie as they entered the ballroom. In awe of the splendor, they looked like two fish out of water as Dottie sweetly reminded them to close their mouths. The entourage had spent all afternoon at the nail and hair salon where much laughter and primping had been had. Isabel had chosen a sleek, black, mid-length dress. The satin complimented her curves in all the right places. Olivia had chosen a silver-grey satin dress that hugged her body like an old friend. Ms. Dottie was decked out in an elegant gold gown and assured the girls they looked pleasingly lovely.

It was apparent this wasn't Dottie's first time at the ball. She waved, nodded and smiled at other patrons as they were led to the table she had purchased for the evening. Izzy couldn't help but notice the décor that enveloped the room. Tall centerpieces captured your attention and were filled with fresh flowers that created an aroma throughout the room. Everything seemed to sparkle on the table. Boxes laid nicely in front of every plate as take-away mementos for the guests. The girls did their best not to stare, but the sheer elegance of the room nearly took their breath away.

Arriving at the table, Isabel quickly noticed they weren't Ms. Dottie's only guests. Sebastian and Chance stood as the ladies arrived at their seats. Sebastian looked dashing in his tuxedo, smelling of citrus with a hint of sweet. His tan skin appeared striking against the white of his shirt and his slicked back raven hair. Izzy realized she had never seen Bash this dressed up. She didn't even know he owned a tux. When he caught her staring he smiled, then swiftly scooted around the table to hold out the chair for Ms. Dottie and then Isabel.

Pushing in Izzy's chair, Bash leaned down and whispered in her ear, "you look ravishing."

Izzy tried hard not to blush and looked around the room attempting to hide her embarrassment.

"You look beautiful, Liv," Chance said loud enough for everyone at the table to hear.

"Thanks Chance," replied Olivia with a smile. "You clean up pretty nice yourself."

"See how easy that was?" grinned Sebastian as he gave Isabel a little wink.

The night was filled with one course after another. Izzy found it hard to concentrate on eating when there was people watching to be done. She could spot the real old money people who attended. There was almost an air about them reminding everyone around that they were just a little bit better than the average Joe. It took great restraint to keep from erupting in laughter. Isabel wasn't one to put on airs and she got a kick out of others who felt they needed to.

"Well, I wondered if this little group would be here this evening," purred Emma as she reached their table. She was dressed in a deep royal blue gown that complimented her eyes and accentuated her blonde hair. Izzy had no idea she would be here tonight, and it put a burr under her saddle. She couldn't help but wonder if Emma was *always* going to be around?

"I just popped over to remind you to leave a spot on your dance card for me," she declared looking directly at Sebastian.

On that note, Sebastian rose to his feet and extended his hand to Isabel. "Sorry Emma. I'm afraid my dance card is already full tonight," replied Bash in a matter-of-fact tone. "Shall we?"

Izzy was so taken aback with the gesture that she took Sebastian's hand and followed him to the dance floor. Emma stood staring after them with a snarl curling her lips.

"You didn't need to do that," declared Isabel. "You know she's going to be mad at you for embarrassing her."

"Do I look worried?" asked Sebastian displaying a face of calm resolve. "Besides, I was being serious. There's no other woman in this room I want to dance with except you. Maybe it's time I made that clear."

His eyes bore a hole into hers. He drew her closer. It was unnerving to stand this near to Bash. His arm was woven tightly around her waist, his hand held hers with a gentle touch and she could feel his breath on her neck. Isabel tried to pull back, but his grip never relented.

"I know you're afraid Iz," whispered Sebastian in her ear. "But please don't pull away from this. Don't pull away from me."

She contemplated his request and then gradually began to relax in his arms. She knew how hard Sebastian was trying to win back her trust. She wanted to trust him and wished they could find their way back to where they were a year ago. But trust didn't come easy for Isabel, and every time Bash tried to get close, her instinct to run would kick back in.

When the dance ended, instead of escorting Izzy back to the table to join the others, Bash slid her hand in the crook of his arm and quietly led her outside. The waiters handed each of them a mint julep, a traditional cocktail for this event, Sebastian explained. They walked silently for a while, sipping their drinks and staring out at the bay. Lights were strung in the big oaks that outlined the property, and Isabel remembered they had been together on a night just like this not that long ago.

"Doesn't this remind you of the street party we attended on Ms. Dottie's street?" asked Izzy with a thoughtful smile on her face.

"I thought you looked so pretty that night, under the sparkling trees, dancing with me," replied Bash. "I didn't think anything could top that night, but I was wrong." He stopped so he could look directly at Izzy. He tucked a stray hair behind her ear that had escaped from her updo. As his hand brushed against her cheek, she felt electricity shoot through her body. Bash leaned down and kissed her. Isabel didn't pull away but leaned even closer, letting Sebastian engulf her in his arms. For just one night, Izzy wanted to feel the love they once shared and to let all her inhibitions go. She didn't want to think about what could go wrong or the risk of getting hurt.

Sebastian grabbed her hand and entwined his fingers through hers. They strolled along the walkway, enjoying the night air and stars, until they had made their way back towards the ballroom. As they entered the room, a young gentleman approached Isabel and asked if he could have the next dance. Izzy looked at the young gentleman and then back at Sebastian. Politely she answered, "I'm sorry. I'm afraid my dance card is alrighty full tonight." She smiled up at Sebastian and placed her hand in the crook of his arm. He placed his hand over hers and smiling, led her towards the dance floor.

Chapter 20

"Okay, enough is enough," declared Olivia as she entered Izzy's office and found her staring out the window. "I've found you like this every day this week. What is going on?"

"I don't know what you're talking about," replied Izzy. "It's beautiful outside. So, I'm staring."

"And I would say that was normal, if I was the one doing it," admitted Olivia. "But this isn't normal for *you*."

Isabel had spent the past week mulling over the events of the Grand Ball. It was nice to just let go and not overthink every moment with Sebastian. It felt wonderful to be securely in his arms again and paraded around the ball as if they belonged together. But she had already walked this path with Bash. Then he walked away and vanished. She was left with a broken heart that hadn't yet healed, and now found herself back in the same predicament. How could she ever trust him again? That was not an easy question to answer.

And then there was her stalker. He was starting to really unnerve her. Izzy had purposefully dropped a hint around the store one day when she thought she'd figured out who might be trying to torment her. After mentioning she inadvertently sold a favorite book of hers at the spring market, it suddenly turned up from her "secret admirer" and confirmed her suspicions. But how could she prove it to the police?

"Hello?" interrupted Olivia. "So, what do you say?"

"About what?" Izzy hadn't heard a word she said. "I'm sorry. My mind was somewhere else."

"That's a yes then," smiled Olivia. "I'll close up and then we can go."

Trailing Olivia to the front of the store, she realized she'd agreed to closing early and going to visit Woodsbury Plantation. She really had to start listening to what people were saying and stop daydreaming. Izzy had heard a little about this planation since she arrived in town but only from locals chatting about it in the bookstore. She loved when farmers would sell their produce on the side of the road; everything always tasted a little fresher. But Izzy had never been to a pecan orchard. Now that fall was finally here, mid-afternoon wasn't so hot and humid as it is in the summer months. Izzy ran upstairs to get her hat, then her and Olivia were off to play hooky for the rest of the day.

The crowd was minimal when they first arrived. They told the workers they'd like to pick some pecans then visit the market to see what wonderful goodies had been baked to sell. They didn't have to pick up their own pecans; it was just part of the experience and fun.

The plantation had something called a tree shaker that looked like a small bulldozer. Once they had a good number of people out in the orchard ready to pick nuts, the tree shaker would ram up against the tree and shake it vigorously. It looked like it was raining pecans, and if you were standing too close, you might get hit in the head. Once the shaking stopped, everyone nearby would fill their baskets with pecans. Isabel and Olivia were laughing so hard at one another tears streamed down their faces.

After Izzy had gathered all she needed, she decided to wander through the orchard. They had areas that had been fenced off, and not too far away were cows eating hay in a field. Isabel leaned up against the fence post and gazed out at the rich green grass that covered the mass expanse. Some of the cows were cooling off in a pond nearby while one mama cow was feeding her baby.

Music could be heard hovering close by. Izzy meandered her way back towards the melodious sound.

"Aren't they great?" asked Olivia when Isabel finally joined her.

"You knew there was going to be a band, in the middle of a

planation, having a concert?" asked Izzy a little confused.

"Of course," answered Olivia as she swayed to the music. "Woodsbury Plantation has what they call 'Autumn Nights' this time of year."

"Oh, sure," Izzy laughed at her bubbly young friend. "I don't know why I wouldn't know that."

The oaks that covered the property provided plenty of shade as people gathered around. Some had brought lawn chairs; others were sitting on blankets. Benches were provided up closer to the stage, but the girls decided to take shelter on the lush grass provided under a tall oak. The breeze was mild but refreshing, and the tree provided shade from the afternoon sun. Isabel was so happy they had come. A day spent outside really refreshed her mind and body.

"Hey girls," blurted out Chance disrupting the solitude. "Sorry we're late."

Izzy glanced over to see Chance give Olivia a peck on the cheek. What did he mean by "we?"

"Good evening ladies," came the all too familiar voice. "I stopped by one of the food trucks to grab us some drinks."

Apparently, Liv had made quite a few assumptions about tonight without telling her.

"Where have you been?" asked Sebastian. "I've been by the bookstore several times this week to talk, but every time I came

Olivia said you were in your office and didn't want to be disturbed."

"I've had a lot to work through," hesitated Izzy. "I just needed some time alone to figure some things out."

"I'm sorry I haven't been able to stay at your apartment this week," began Bash. "I've had some business with renters and charters, and I didn't want to wake you coming in late. But I'll be back tonight."

Izzy got up and walked towards the field. Bash followed quickly behind to see what was wrong.

"Look Bash," started Izzy. "I appreciate all you've done to help me. I can only imagine how much pain your back has been in sleeping on that couch all this time. You've been so sweet and protective." Isabel only stopped a moment to see his reaction and then continued. "I've been doing a lot of thinking and I'm going to tell Ms. Dottie I will stay through the end of the year, but then she will need to find someone else to run the bookstore."

Sebastian stopped walking and just stared at her; or maybe he was staring through her. Whatever it was, it made Izzy very uncomfortable. Then he abruptly turned and walked back to join Chance and Olivia.

Not knowing what to do with herself, Isabel wandered over to the market to peruse all the homemade goodies that were being sold. Pecan pies, pecan bars, pecan cookies, pecan nut butter, butter pecan cake…if the word pecan was in the title, it was there. Izzy loved homemade goodies but limited herself to only buying a few of the sweets.

"You're running and you know it," declared Bash. "You're running from me. From us."

Izzy whipped around when she heard Sebastian's voice. Grabbing him by the arm she escorted him out of the store and away from curious ears.

"I wanted to tell you before I told Ms. Dottie," replied Izzy. "I wanted you to hear it from me. And I'm not running. You told me not too long ago I would have to make a decision and I have."

Sebastian was quiet for a long time. He knew she was afraid of loving him again and after the Grand Ball he knew she did. It was evident in how she responded to his words, his touch. Bash longed to make her feel secure in their relationship again, in his love for her. He had until the end of the year, not to just tell her, but to show her.

Chapter 21

Isabel could hardly believe it was October. She just loved fall and the activities that came with it. School was well under way; football games were being played and bonfires roared with an open invitation to cozy up and roast some marshmallows. Leaves were always a little late to the party in the deep south, but they eventually showed off their brilliant colors, eventually covering the ground once their beauty had faded. Izzy always felt so exhilarated this time of year knowing the heat would eventually subside and give everyone a much-needed break.

Izzy still needed to talk to Ms. Dottie and let her know her long-range plans. She hated to abandon her sweet friend, who was more like a grandmother, but she could see no other way to protect her heart than to leave the sweet little town of Fairhope. The longer she stayed, the more convinced she became if she stuck around too long, Sebastian would eventually find a way to break her heart again, and that wasn't an option.

However, she was here now and wanted to do everything

she could to leave the bookstore in tip-top shape for Ms. Dottie in case she decided to make a go of it and keep it open. Izzy spent time to preparing the store for one of the big weekends ahead, Fairhope's famous Witches' Parade. It was a signature Halloween tradition for the town, consisting of hundreds of costumed witches competing in a 13-mile bike race to raise money for the animal rescue shelter. Family and friends gathered to support the participants as they biked in their varying costumes.

Izzy decided to decorate the store for the holiday to gain more business during the packed parade. While hanging up floating ghosts across the bookcase, the bell rang announcing the arrival of their first customer of the day. When Izzy glanced up, she caught sight of Bash entering the store.

"Good morning ladies," sang Sebastian. "I come bearing gifts." He was carrying two coffees and a bag full of goodies that he placed on the counter. "I wanted to stop by and invite you girls to join a group of us that are going to the Autumn Daze Corn Maize. We go every year and I thought ya'll might like to come along."

Olivia squealed in delight. "That sounds awesome Bash. Is Chance going?"

"Of course, he's going," replied Bash. "I wouldn't leave him out of all the fun."

"Well, I'm in," smiled Olivia, taking her coffee and sweet

treat to enjoy alone while the two love birds stood in awkward silence.

"So, what do you say Iz," asked Sebastian not sure how she would answer. "I know how much you love fall activities."

Isabel's mind was already at work devising up an idea. "Sure," she answered. "But I have a small favor to ask." Sebastian looked curious so she continued. "Will you invite Tristan to come along?"

The twitch in Bash's cheek let her know he wasn't happy about her request, so she quickly explained.

"It's nothing like you're thinking," explained Isabel. "I just need him there to prove something. That's all I'm going to say for now."

Sebastian gave her a quizzical look then agreed to invite him to come along. Whatever Izzy had up her sleeve, she obviously wasn't going to share with him. He wondered if having Tristan along would cause a distraction for Isabel. He had hoped they could spend some time together. Sebastian didn't think she had changed her mind about dating Tristan, but she was definitely up to something.

****

The farm with the maize was located just outside of Fairhope. Izzy had no idea there would-be other activities on the property. They offered hayrides along with bonfires where visitors huddled around the flames, roasting marshmallows. A small petting zoo with some of the farm animals was set up for kids to enjoy. Games like horseshoes and cornhole were placed in several spots outside of the maize for those who preferred a different kind of entertainment. A local country band was playing old school classics, providing the perfect cozy ambience to compliment the fall evening.

Sebastian and Izzy arrived at the maize, joined by an eclectic group: Asher, Emma, Tristan and even a few other old friends were invited to the outing. Izzy noticed Tristan chatting with people from the town, people he'd known his entire life. Oliva and Chance were just walking up to join the group when she spotted Izzy and gave her a big smile and waved. Isabel waved back and headed straight to the line so she could go in first. They allowed one or two people to go at a time in order to keep the maize from getting jammed up.

Sebastian scanned the crowd and saw Isabel standing at the front of the line to the maize. Before her name could escape his lips, she disappeared inside. His big plan for spending time with Izzy just came to a screeching halt. The rest of the group headed towards the maize and each started their journey when given the nod by the attendant. Laughter and yelling could be heard throughout the thick stalks of corn as each person or couple wove their way within the giant puzzle. Scarecrows were placed at strategic spots all throughout the different paths, holding a sign that spurred you on.

One particular scarecrow stood out and didn't fit the pattern, causing several people to stop and ponder what the sign could mean. The scarecrow, dressed in a nightgown blowing in the autumn wind, held a worn wooden sign with the words painted "I know what you've done" across the front. People weren't sure if it was meant to scare them or detour them from the correct path, but eventually would give up and just move along. That is, all but one maize participant.

As he arrived in front of the scarecrow, shock travelled all throughout his body. He stood there, frozen in place, staring in disbelief. The color in his face vanished, and his eyes darted back and forth fearing what might happen next. He lifted the sign to see if there was anything else written to elaborate on the message. Finally, Isabel stepped from the shadows.

"What are you doing here?" he asked with a quiver in his voice.

"I might ask the same thing of you, Asher," came the retort.

"I'm going through the maize just like you," he tried to explain with very little conviction.

"I saw your expression, Asher," came the biting response from Izzy. "When you saw *my* nightgown on the scarecrow, the same one that was stolen out of my apartment, and read the sign, your face gave you away."

"I don't know what you are talking about," he replied with a quiver in his voice. "I was just shocked to see a nightgown on a scarecrow."

"Come clean or I will call the police right now and turn you in," Isabel spoke through clenched teeth trying to keep from yelling. "I bought another nightgown, just like the one that was stolen out of my apartment, to try and catch the culprit tonight. I had no idea that person would be you. My stalker."

Sebastian rounded the corner just in time to hear the words "my stalker."

"What about your stalker," asked Bash as he interrupted the conversation, "and what in the world is on that Scarecrow?"

Asher was shifting on his feet, appearing extremely antsy.

"Asher is my stalker," replied Isabel in a biting tone. "I just caught him red-handed. I bought a replica of my nightgown that was stolen and put it on this Scarecrow. I wanted to flush out my stalker tonight and it appears I did."

"Is that true Asher?" Bash asked in disbelief. "Have you been sending Izzy all those weird gifts?" He was trying to keep his anger in check. After all, this was one of his best friends. Surely, he wouldn't do something so nefarious.

Asher exploded in frustration. "I did it for you Bash," yelled Asher. "I couldn't stand by and watch Izzy hurt you again. I know what that feels like and I couldn't let it happen, so I tried to scare her into leaving town."

Isabel stood speechless. She didn't know how to respond to something so hateful by someone she thought she knew so well. She had asked Bash to invite Tristan along thinking he was the offender; she was not prepared to find out it was Asher. Glancing over at Bash, she saw the muscle in his cheek twitching and knew he was a volcano just waiting to erupt. Isabel grabbed his arm and asked if he'd help her get out of the maize. They both needed to cool off before discussing this any further.

Turning to leave, Izzy stopped and fumed at Asher, "This isn't over. I just can't look at you right now."

They walked in silence until they found the exit out of the maize, both consumed with what just happened.

Chapter 22

By the next week, it seemed everyone in town had heard about the stunt Asher had pulled with Isabel. Not because she was telling anyone. It only takes a few people to know in a small town before rumors begin to spread; everyone knows everyone else's business. Izzy was still in shock from it all and had laid low trying to busy herself with the store and adding last minute touches for Halloween.

Today was the Witches' Parade, and Isabel solely wanted to forget all of her problems for a few hours and enjoy the event. She had to leave it to this small town she'd come to love; they all knew how to enjoy themselves. The ladies that dressed as witches expressed themselves in all kinds of crazy fashion, from the Wicked Witch of the West, to orange, purple and pink haired witches sporting fish net stockings. Some witches were in tutus, some sparkled in Mardi Gras costumes while others displayed Halloween paraphernalia hanging off their body, providing an awe-inducing spectacle.

"Earth to Izzy," whispered Sebastian. "Can I talk to you a

minute?

"Hi," she replied. "Sorry, I didn't see you coming."

"I didn't want to interrupt you enjoying the parade but was wondering if we could talk for a few minutes."

"Sure," she replied. "Let's step back a little from the street so I can actually hear you."

"I'm sorry I haven't come over the last few days," Bash continued. "I had to get my head on straight and then have a conversation with Asher."

Isabel flinched at the mention of his name. She had been mulling over that scene at the corn maize a million times, and still was in shock over his behavior. How could someone she once dated, even loved, do something so horrible to her? Had she really been that nasty of a person to deserve something like this?

"I'm surprised the two of you are talking," said Isabel, completely unemotional. "I figured there might be some punching but not necessarily talking." She smiled in spite of her pain.

"I thought about it, trust me. But he and I needed to talk, or we would never be friends again."

"Would that be so bad?" Isabel smirked, knowing that wasn't the answer he wanted to hear.

"You need to talk to him Iz," came the reply that was almost a whisper. Sebastian knew he might get slapped for that suggestion, so he braced himself for the worst.

It was Izzy's turn to be livid. Why in the world would she subject herself to talking with Asher? He didn't deserve a conversation as far as she was concerned. The past was the past and if he couldn't leave it there, then there was nothing she could do about it now. How could Sebastian ask her to talk to him?

"I'm not interested in a conversation with him right now," replied Isabel. "And if that's all you came to talk about, I'd really like to get back to the parade." Isabel walked away never looking back to see Sebastian's reaction.

The day ended up being a welcome distraction, and Izzy returned to the bookstore happy and exhausted. Locking the door, she headed upstairs in hopes of a warm, sudsy bath to soothe her sore muscles. As she neared the top of the stairs, a silhouette could be spotted in the corner. Izzy froze in place not knowing whether to attack or run.

"I just want to talk," said Asher as he stepped from the shadows. "I knew you would say no if I asked beforehand, so I've been waiting for you to come home."

"You don't think you've already scared me enough? Now you're hiding in the shadows. Besides, I don't have anything to say to you," she snapped. "I don't even know *what* to say to you." She brushed past him and unlocked the door.

"You don't have to say anything," replied Asher. "I'll do the talking."

In spite of her reservations, she left the door ajar and Asher followed her inside.

"I would need to see a therapist for several months before I could totally explain my recent actions," explained Asher. "When I saw you over a year ago, I was so happy to reconnect with you and for us to be able to sort through the past and become friends." Asher sat down on one of the antique chair's while Isabel stood, staring out the window. "Then you and Bash got together, and I was really happy for both of you. But when you guys broke up his heart was crushed. I had to watch him mope around, and I guess it brought back a lot of bad memories." Asher's face crumbled in a pained expression. "Memories of when you broke up with me. I started reliving things I thought I had let go of a long time ago, and I didn't want to see my best friend go through the same thing." Asher stopped to take a breath and tried to read Isabel's reaction so far. She appeared to be listening, even though her back was turned away from him.

"Did you forget how long it took me to trust you all those years we dated?" asked Isabel. "It will take me much longer to forget about this. Your excuses just aren't good enough. But I guess you'll be happy to know that I'm leaving at the end of the year. Isn't that what you wanted?"

Asher cradled his head in his handles, overwhelmed with

feelings of guilt and remorse. Isabel walked over, grabbed his hands and made him look at her.

"And why would you break into my apartment and steal a nightgown?" asked Izzy in a quizzical tone.

"I broke in thinking I would take something small. I wasn't sure what to take and while searching for something personal I decided to make a mess. One thing led to another and I figured a nightgown was about as personal of an item as I could take." Asher sounded frustrated with himself. "I am truly sorry Iz. I don't know what I was thinking. I guess I wasn't."

A knock interrupted the moment and Isabel hesitated on whether to answer or not. Sebastian's voice could be heard on the other side of the door as he continued to knock frantically. Isabel rushed to the door to let him in.

"Sorry to barge in but I need to talk to you," declared Sebastian as he entered the apartment spotting Asher on the sofa. "And it needs to be alone."

Izzy couldn't figure out what was so important it couldn't wait. Wasn't he the one who asked her to talk to Asher? She wasn't sure if she would ever understand this complex man. Asher didn't argue and got up to leave as requested.

"I want to finish our talk later Izzy," said Asher before he turned and left.

"I'm sorry for interrupting like that," said Bash. "But I

needed to tell you something."

"What's wrong with you Sebastian?" asked Izzy. "You're acting strange."

Sebastian took her hands in his. "I received a call tonight from Ms. Dottie's attorney." He paused to gather himself, hoping she would see his care for her. "He called to tell me Ms. Dottie passed away in her sleep last night. She had a stroke."

Silence filled the small apartment. Izzy couldn't move. Surely, she had misunderstood what Sebastian just said. She had just spent a whole day with Ms. Dottie getting ready for the Grand Ball. They had laughed, primped and talked just like they had done on so many occasions before. Ms. Dottie had never looked more beautiful than the night of the ball. A southern lady of pure elegance. She couldn't be gone. She just couldn't be. Izzy sat completely still as a calm numbness overtook her body.

Chapter 23

The sunshine sparkled through the apartment window, sprinkling drops of light all about the room. As the warmth touched Isabel's face, she stirred in bed with a lazy yawn. Stretching her arms high above her head, she bumped a large object that was lying next to her. She glanced over to see Sebastian, fully dressed, taking up occupancy on the other side of her bed. Glancing down, she observed she too was fully dressed and suddenly recalled the events of the evening before.

Used tissue was crumpled and scattered around the room, reminding Izzy of her unexpected grief. She laid there, looking up at the ceiling and wishing she could go back to sleep and pretend it was all a horrible dream. When Sebastian began to stir, she was quickly reminded she was fully awake.

"Good morning," whispered Bash in the softest voice possible, as if he could break Izzy with his voice alone.

"Hi," was all Izzy could muster. She quickly scooted out of bed to assess her appearance. When she saw her reflection in a nearby mirror the best description would be "The Night of the Living Dead." Mascara had run down and puddled under her eyes, not a stitch of makeup was left on her face and her nose was red from the constant blowing. Her hair looked like Don King's, standing straight up all over her head.

"You were a wreck last night," declared Sebastian. "I stayed to..."

"...bring me comfort? I remember," stated Izzy with tears in her eyes. "Thank you for that. I don't think I could have made it if I had been left alone."

Bash stood up and came over to her. "I would do anything for you Iz. Anything." He wrapped his arms around her. He loved being able to offer her a shoulder to cry on and bring comfort during her time of grief.

"I was so upset last night I forgot to ask," started Izzy. "Why would Ms. Dottie's attorney call you? How did he even know who you were?"

"Sorry. I meant to explain that to you last night, but you were so upset I didn't want to get into it just yet," answered Bash. "After you left a year ago, Ms. Dottie called and asked me to come over. When I arrived, her attorney was there. She wanted to know if I would be the executor over her will. With no husband or children still alive, she needed someone she could trust and lived close by."

Isabel took a moment to really look at Sebastian. He was one of the most caring and protective people she had ever known. He had always taken care of her when they were together and now, she found out he was taking care of someone she loved. Izzy leaned over and gently kissed him.

"Thank you for caring for me and Ms. Dottie," she looked down, not being able to make eye contact with his chestnut eyes.

Sebastian tipped her chin up and ran his thumb against her cheek. "I said I would do anything for you Iz. Anything." Bash's phone rang, interrupting the moment. He stepped away to take the call.

Isabel watched as he chatted on the phone. She had looked into Sebastian's eyes many times since returning to Alabama, but for the first time she could see his pain. Pain over her. Pain over their breakup. But she also saw his love for her. Maybe they could start from the pain and build from there.

"That was Ms. Dottie's attorney," said Bash. "He asked if you and I could meet with him today. I asked him if 1:00 would be convenient. Is that time okay with you?"

"Of course," answered Izzy. "But why does he need to meet with me?"

"I'm not sure of everything that's listed in her will," he replied. "We went over a few things of the bigger things but not everything. I didn't even know about the bookstore until she asked me if I could deliver that furniture here."

Sebastian asked if she would be okay for a few hours and went home to get cleaned up. After Izzy got dressed, she went downstairs to make arrangements with Olivia for the rest of the day. When she told Liv of Ms. Dottie's passing, the poor young girl broke into sobs. They had only been together a few times, but like most people the kind woman encountered, Olivia had formed an instant friendship and admiration for the older lady.

****

When they arrived at the attorney's office, Bash and Izzy sat silent in the car trying to gather themselves before going inside. Once entering, an elderly gentleman named Walter Brown greeted them and led them back to his office. Walter sat himself down behind a worn mahogany desk and gestured for his guests to settle into the adjacent leather chairs.

Wanting to make his guests feel comfortable, Walter shared some personal information about himself. He told them he was semi-retired now and only came into the office three days a week to do paperwork. Walter had been close friends with Dottie's husband and after he passed away, he had become close friends with Dottie.

"As you know Sebastian, she asked you to be the executor of her will," stated Walter. "But I will let you know that Dottie has already taken care of most of the arrangements, and this is mainly a formality."

Walter brought out forms that needed to be signed and had Sebastian look over papers to understand Ms. Dottie's desires and wishes.

Once Bash had finished his official duties and discussed final arrangements, Walter looked up at Isabel who had been extremely quiet during the process.

"Dottie spoke of you so often, Isabel," said Walter with an endearing tone. "As you probably know, she loved you like a daughter. She left me something to read to you." Walter pulled out a letter from the file he'd been going through with Bash. Isabel reached over and grabbed Sebastian's hand.

Walter began. "My dear Ms. Isabel, if Walter is reading you this letter then you know I've left my earthly home. I want you to know how much I love you honey. You were like a breath of fresh air the day you walked into my life."

Izzy began to sob thinking about her dear friend who had taken her into her home and into her life. Sebastian squeezed her hand, reminding her she could lean on him.

"From the first time you walked through my door, you held such a special place in my heart. I don't have many things that are highly valuable, but anything you might want in the house is yours. Make sure Sebastian lets you walk through before giving everything else to charity. And one last thing sweetie. From the day my sister passed away, I had Walter put the bookstore in your name. I don't know how you feel about that, but it's your decision to make going forward. I sure will miss that cute smile, but I know we will see each other again."

Tears were flowing freely down Izzy's face. Walter handed her some tissues and then had her sign some papers. Ms. Dottie had taken care of every detail she could beforehand, and it didn't take much time to wrap up the rest of the business.

When Bash and Izzy reached the door, Walter stopped them with one final thought. "Dottie talked about the two of you quite often," he said. "She hoped the bookstore would bring you two back together."

Sebastian winked at Izzy and smiled. "She can't help but be a matchmaker even from beyond."

Chapter 24

When Walter Brown read Ms. Dottie's will, it was revealed she didn't want a funeral. All of her family members had passed away and there were only a handful of friends still alive. Bash and Izzy shared a few personal words at her graveside and said their goodbyes. As they climbed in the car, Sebastian asked if they could drive by Ms. Dottie's house to check on everything and ask one of her neighbors to keep an eye on the place. Walter and Bash knew Ms. Dottie wanted to donate her house to the Azalea Trail Organization and said they could use it however they felt necessary. Before she passed, she suggested to the organization the possibility of converting it into a tearoom for the girls.

Turning onto Ms. Dottie's street, they could see cars lined up on both sides of the road. Sebastian slowly maneuvered his way through the cars and pulled into her driveway. As they were walking to the door, a few people that had been waiting got out of their cars to come and greet them. They were mostly older friends of Dottie's who had come to pay their respects. When asked if they were family, Bash and Izzy explained it wasn't by blood, but in all other ways they were definitely family. Some folks were still in their cars, not able to make the walk, so Bash and Izzy went to them and expressed their appreciation for dropping by to pay their respects.

Ms. Dottie's friends ranged from old Mobile society to everyday people she had befriended along the way. Sebastian recognized a few familiar faces, and they shared stories about Ms. Dottie with one another. Isabel stood back quietly and observed. When she was growing up in Mobile, southern ladies knew just what to do at a funeral. While the family grieved, the ladies would bring casseroles, desserts, ham or chicken to make sure the family would have plenty to eat. They would busy themselves catering to guests that dropped by so the family didn't have anything to worry about. But today, there were no family members present and the people who dropped by were all Ms. Dottie's closest friends. Everyone seemed a little lost on how to handle the situation.

Isabel was standing on the porch when a single mom introduced herself and told her of the time Ms. Dottie had made the Azalea Trail dress for her daughter and didn't charge her anything. She knew how expensive the whole process could be and wanted to help. It wasn't hard for Izzy to believe the story. Ms.

Dottie had a heart of gold.

The porch was full of flowers and plants that had been dropped off by friends. Izzy spotted some yellow Gerber Daisies by the door and smiled knowing those were some of Ms. Dottie's favorite flowers. As she continued watching, a young lady approached the porch and pinned a lilac ribbon on the wreath hanging on the front door. It was already overflowing with multiple-colored ribbons. When the young lady noticed Izzy watching she explained about the wreath.

"Word spread on social media about Ms. Dottie passing away. She had made so many girls dresses as an Azalea Trail Maid that they wanted to honor her by doing something special. They each cut a piece off the bottom hem of their dress to make a ribbon to attach to the wreath."

Izzy wiped away a tear as Sebastian walked up to take her hand. He unlocked the door and they stepped inside. At that moment the past flooded into the present. She glanced through the doorway, half expecting to see Ms. Dottie coming out of the kitchen to greet them wearing a smile and apron.

Izzy could almost smell breakfast cooking as she entered the kitchen, running her hand along the worn countertop. They had sat right here on many mornings sharing coffee and biscuits.

As they continued to walk through the house, it already felt like a museum. While always immaculate, it appeared as if she had gone to extra lengths to have everything just right. Each room held its own special memory for Izzy. She hesitated outside of Ms. Dottie's bedroom, as if entering it would be disturbing some sacred place.

Isabel walked through the room, observing every small detail. When she glanced at the nightstand, she spotted the string of pearls Dottie had worn the first time they met. She picked them up and held them in her hand, rubbing each bead with her finger as if praying the rosary.

"You need to take those Iz," suggested Sebastian as he slipped up behind her. "She would want you to have them."

"I can't," stammered Isabel. "It wouldn't be right."

"Southern moms and grandmas hand down their pearls to their daughters and granddaughters all the time," replied Bash with an assuring tone. "Dottie always thought of you as a daughter. Especially since her daughter had passed away." Sebastian picked up the pearls and gently eased them around Izzy's neck. She couldn't help but reach up and touch them, hoping to feel closer to her sweet old friend.

Bash and Izzy were exhausted when they finally decided to

head back to Fairhope. It had been a long emotional day. When they arrived at the bookstore, Isabel wasn't ready to go inside quite yet, so they walked around back towards the bay. Water was a soothing element and she needed something to settle her unrest. They walked in silence along the bayfront hoping the sights and sounds would ease their minds.

It wasn't long before Izzy headed towards her favorite spot. The bench behind the bookstore that overlooked the bay. Her place of solace.

"Do you mind if I spend some time alone?" she asked Bash.

"I really don't think you need to stay alone tonight," replied Sebastian in an over-protective tone.

"I don't want to argue," countered Izzy. "So, let's strike a truce. Go on ahead of me and I'll meet you at your place a little later. I think I'd rather sleep at your apartment anyway."

Sebastian was a little surprised but kissed her on the forehead, turned to leave, then spun back around to smile back at her. She forced a smile hoping to convince him she'd be alright. Isabel felt anything but alright. Her heart and mind were flooded with emotions and feelings. A couple of days ago she was planning on leaving Fairhope at the end of the year and putting all of this behind her. Now her world had been rocked.

Watching Bash walk away, she knew he was the cause of her confusion. He was the source of her anxiety, the cause of her pain. Yet he was her rock that made everything bearable. Bash had made it clear that he wanted a second chance and so far, had lived up to that promise. Yet she couldn't forget all that transpired between them in their past relationship. How long before he decided it was too much work or he just walked away? Izzy knew she couldn't go through all of that again, but she was confused by her own feelings. She still cared very deeply for him. Just a few days ago when she finally made the decision to leave, there was a feeling of relief. Now her uncertainty had returned, and Izzy felt like she was right back where she started. Looking at the empty bench seat next to her, she wished she could see Ms. Dottie's smiling face, telling her it would all be alright and easing her anxiety in the way she always knew how.

Chapter 25

It had been several weeks since Ms. Dottie's funeral. Isabel had met with an accountant to discuss ownership of Bayfront Books. It was one thing to manage a bookstore and take care of the bills, it was another thing entirely to be an owner. At first Izzy was overwhelmed with the thought of owning anything. Would she decide to stay in Fairhope and run the store? Would she stay the owner and just hire someone to manage the day-to-day business? Would she sell it? That thought quickly came off the "what will I do" list. The thought that Ms. Dottie loved and trusted her enough to leave her the family business was awe-inspiring. The pride she felt would not allow her to sell the bookstore. Isabel would do her very best to make it a success. If she decided somewhere down the road to sell it, it would only be when the bookstore was a huge success.

Ever since the funeral, Izzy had opted to sleep at Sebastian's. She found her favorite spot on the porch, opened up the sliding windows and fell asleep every night with the bay crashing against the marina. Bash had given her space and let her mourn in her own way. He was usually up and out on the dock way before she woke up. He always had a pot of hot coffee waiting when she finally pulled herself out of bed.

This morning she found a note by her mug letting her know Bash would be helping the Coast Guard and wouldn't be home until much later. Of course, he begged her to come over early because storms were coming in and they were expecting massive flooding. As Isabel sipped her coffee, she went to the porch and looked out at the sky. Gray, rolling clouds hung low in the atmosphere over the water. She quickly gathered her stuff together in order to beat the downpour that was soon to follow.

After a hasty shower back at her place, she dressed in a flash and was downstairs ready to open right on time. Olivia walked in soaked to the bone.

"Oh, my word," exclaimed Olivia as she entered the bookstore drenched. "The roads leading into town are already showing signs of flooding."

"Bash left me a note this morning saying a big storm was supposed to be coming through," replied Isabel, looking out the window to watch the downpour.

"This morning, huh?" came the quizzical response. "Are you

still staying at Sebastian's place?" Olivia couldn't help but smile at her annoyed friend.

"I didn't agree to discuss that," quipped Izzy. "Besides, I wanted us to discuss my plans going forward with the bookstore."

"So, you decided to keep it?" squealed Olivia clapping in delight. "I was hoping you would, but I didn't want to influence you either way."

Isabel and Olivia sat down for the next few hours to discuss some of her ideas. It was important for Izzy to keep the shop as quaint as possible, but she wanted to add activities that would bring in more customers. A reading corner would be sat up in the back and every Tuesday morning she wanted to have a reading circle for little kids. They could take turns reading and could even have special guests invited to share stories. As they talked and planned, Izzy was exhilarated with the prospect of keeping the old traditions of Bayfront Books, but also adding in some of her new ideas. The day flew by as they jotted down notes and put dates on the calendar. With the storm still raging outside and very little customers roaming about town, Isabel sent Olivia home early and closed the store. She ran upstairs, grabbed a few items of her own and headed for Sebastian's before it grew too dark.

The roads were already flooded as she made her way to the marina. She hoped that Bash had finished early and was already at his apartment waiting for her. Once entering, she realized her hopes were dashed. His place was empty and dark. Izzy flipped on the lights and TV to see where the storm was headed and how much longer it planned on raining. The weatherman didn't sound very promising.

She nervously paced throughout the apartment. She picked up a shirt Bash had left lying on the bed that still carried the smell of his aftershave. Her heart ached for them to be back together. How long would she allow her fear of the unknown to control her? Sebastian's presence in her life made her feel afraid and safe at the same time.

Izzy roamed about the enclosed porch. The rain beat against the windows and echoed throughout the empty apartment. Where was Bash? What was taking him so long? Was he safe? He should have been home by now.

"Hey Iz," whispered Sebastian as he opened the door and saw her standing on the porch. "I thought for sure you would be in bed by now."

"Thank heavens," exclaimed Izzy as she ran to him and wrapped both arms around his neck. "I have been worried sick about you."

"You're getting sopping wet, Iz," replied Bash trying to push her away from his saturated body.

"I don't care," she said holding on tighter. "Just hold me, will you?"

Sebastian had no idea what was going on, but this hadn't been the reception he'd received from Izzy over the past few months. She was clinging so tightly to him he thought he might have to peel her off.

"What's wrong?" asked Bash in his most tender voice pushing her hair away from her face. "You're trembling. And I'm not complaining, but you haven't hugged me like that since we were dating."

Isabel finally pulled away but kept holding Bash's hand. "I can't lose someone else right now. I just can't." Soft sobs took over her body as she collapsed into Sebastian's arms.

He tipped her chin until her eyes met his. "You are never going to lose me again." He kissed her on the forehead. "Do you hear me Iz? I'm not going anywhere." Bash kissed her softly on the lips. Her mouth parted to the warmth of his. Izzy pulled him close this time, holding on tight, letting go of all her apprehensions.

Sebastian sat her on the sofa while he went to change out of his wet clothes. Upon returning, he found Izzy curled up in a blanket. Bash pulled her into his arms and gently stroked her hair until she finally fell asleep. He couldn't change their past, but he would do everything possible to change their future.

Chapter 26

Izzy could hardly believe Thanksgiving was tomorrow. Since the day they had laid Ms. Dottie to rest, time had raced by. If it weren't for Olivia's help, the store would have never been decorated. She did a beautiful job and it reminded everyone who walked through the door it was the season to be grateful. She even suggested they give each customer a hot, pumpkin spice latte as they entered the store. Isabel knew Olivia was the perfect employee and was so excited she was here during this growing time for her as a new store owner.

Olivia and Chance were having Thanksgiving lunch at her parents' house and had invited Bash and Isabel to come too. They graciously asked for a rain check, but Bash invited them to come to the marina later in the day for dessert. Sebastian and Izzy were going to eat Thanksgiving lunch at a restaurant, then had plans to go over to Ms. Dottie's house to get any remaining items they might want to keep. The house was being turned over on Monday to the Azalea Trail Society, so they needed to make one last walk through.

At a time when most people are overeating, Izzy found herself pushing her food around on her plate with her mind somewhere else.

"Is the food that bad or am I just bad company?" Bash asked, bringing Izzy back to the present.

"I'm sorry," she stammered, her eyes welling up with tears. "I'm just dreading being back in Ms. Dottie's house with all those memories."

"I know Iz," he replied grabbing her hand across the table. "So, let's just go in and relive the good times. And with today being Thanksgiving, what a great day to be thankful we had the privilege of having this wonderful woman in our lives."

Sebastian held Isabel's hand all the way to the house. It just felt right. Their relationship had grown over the past few weeks and he could feel Izzy's heart opening back up to him. More than anything he wanted to remind her he was here for her no matter what and he wasn't going anywhere.

Isabel slowly ascended the steps to the front porch. The first time she saw this beautiful southern home she fell in love. White rockers sat in twos lining the massive porch. Ferns hung along the front, but their once vibrant leaves were now brown due to lack of care. Izzy ran her hand along the front banister remembering how Ms. Dottie sat on the porch, drinking her sweet tea and hollering out to her as she would be leaving for the evening.

As they entered the house, Isabel could almost hear her friend hollering from the kitchen, "hurry up and get in here Miss City." That's what she always called Isabel. They had spent countless hours in the kitchen. Izzy pulled up a stool to the bar reminiscing about all the cooking lessons at this very spot.

"Do you remember the day you walked in and Dottie was teaching me and a few girls from the Distinguished Young Women's Program about how to make chicken and dumplings?" she asked Sebastian as she was reliving the moment. "You walked over and started interfering with my lesson."

"As I remember it," came Bash's response in a southern drawl, "you were covered in flour and had no idea what you were doing." He chuckled out loud remembering the scene quiet well.

"You walked over and wiped the flour off my cheek," replied Izzy displaying a slight blush. "You totally distracted me from what I was doing."

Bash reached up and caressed her cheek once again. "I can't help I'm a distraction." He smiled in a way that sent Isabel's stomach into a frenzy of somersaults.

Izzy stood and went to a cabinet near the stove. She reached inside and pulled out a big, black iron skillet. "I want to keep this," she remarked. "Ms. Dottie made sausage gravy in this several times a week when I lived here. I loved her biscuits and sausage gravy. Maybe if I use it, I'll learn to be as good a cook as she was one day."

Izzy laid it on the counter then preceded to the bedrooms in the back. There in the sewing room she found patterns and material spread about. It appeared as if Ms. Dottie had been working on someone's dress and everything was just as she left it. Isabel looked in the closet and saw many Azalea Trail dresses hanging inside. She went one by one until she found what she was looking for.

"You looked like a giant pink cupcake in that dress," laughed Sebastian. "I'll never forget walking in, seeing you lose your balance in that contraption and legs were flying amongst a cloud of pink and pantaloons."

Izzy couldn't help but laugh remembering that day. She was so embarrassed in front of Bash and everyone else. She obviously wasn't lady-like enough to be an Azalea Trail Maid. It took a lot of grace to maneuver one of those dresses.

"No worries, I don't plan on wearing it," she replied answering Bash's question before he could ask. "I thought I might have it made into a keepsake. Maybe sown into a quilt or some other kind of keepsake." She wiped away a tear and kept on moving.

Isabel had one last place to look. The small little cottage she had lived in, in back. They passed the patio garden with the gurgling fountain and greenery that surrounded it. This had been such a sweet place for her to come and relax, listen to the water trickle, drink her coffee and let the stress of the day roll off. It had also been the very spot her and Sebastian had declared their love for one another. She couldn't deal with those memories today. This was tough enough and she wanted to get through it as quickly as possible.

She opened the door to the quaint little cottage and memories came flooding back. Not just of Ms. Dottie but Bash too. They had spent many hours in this small, charming house. It appeared to be just as she had left it, with Ms. Dottie not changing a single thing.

"Do you want to know what Ms. Dottie said to me the first day I arrived?" Izzy asked as if speaking to no one in particular. "She threw her arms wide and said, 'Welcome to Dixie honey.' Of course, I reminded her I had lived here before. Then she laughed and told me that Dixie was the name of her estate and she named it that because it was a strong, southern, female name." Isabel took a breath remembering that special day. "She said, just like all us southern gals, this place is a little high maintenance but it's so worth the effort."

Isabel choked up a bit and quickly retreated towards the bedroom. The quilt that had been laying at the foot of the bed when she arrived was still there, so Izzy grabbed it as another item she would like to keep. She turned the corner towards the bathtub and saw the big, clawfoot garden tub she had loved so much.

"I know this probably sounds nutty to you," mumbled Izzy. "But I'd like to have the tub too since I've decided to stay in Fairhope for now. I think I'd like to put it in my new place. I always loved this antique tub." Bash smiled but didn't respond.

Taking her quilt and heading back toward the main house, she noticed Bash stopped when they reached the patio. Isabel turned to see if he had spotted something he would like to keep too.

"Can we just sit out here for a bit?" asked Sebastian looking around the garden. "I always loved this patio and I'd like to sit out here one more time since I won't have the chance to ever again."

Isabel was shocked and frustrated. Didn't he know how much this patio meant to her? Hadn't he found her many times out here when he would stop over? They had shared some serious conversations out on this little piece of heaven. She couldn't just sit out here walking down memory lane with Bash, so Izzy offered to go in and make them a cup of coffee. It was a little nippy outside so it would make perfect sense and Sebastian would never know otherwise. When she returned carrying two piping cups of coffee, she found Bash with his eyes closed. She quietly sat his cup on the table next to him and took a little stroll around the fountain, sipping her hot cup of java. Izzy had loved this patio area when she lived with Ms. Dottie. It had brought her peace when she felt in turmoil, joy when she felt sad, and comfort when she felt lonely.

"Do you remember the street party when you lived here before?" Izzy jumped not realizing Sebastian was fully awake, watching her and sipping his coffee.

"I vaguely remember something like that," she replied trying to sound as nonchalant as possible.

Bash laughed knowing full well she remembered the night of the street party. "Well, let me see if I can refresh your memory. First, we went house to house sampling some delicious food. And if I remember correctly, *someone* downed a glass of what they thought was only lemonade but was spiked with liquor." Bash couldn't control his laughter remembering Izzy coughing and sputtering.

"Oh, and do you remember when we danced under the lights in the street?" asked Bash looking over to see Izzy's reaction.

She had walked to the other side of the fountain trying to put distance between her and Sebastian. Isabel turned her back so he wouldn't see how much this conversation was frustrating her. "Look Bash, I think I've had quite enough of walking down memory lane for today. I'm ready to leave and go back to Fairhope. It's been an emotional day".

Ignoring her, Bash continued. "You ran off after our dance under the lights, with me following close behind. We ended up right here on this patio." Sebastian walked over until he was standing right behind her. "Last time we were here, I told you that I loved you." Bash was practically whispering as he remembered that wonderful night. "This time, I'd like to show you."

Curiosity got the better of Izzy, so she turned to face him. Sebastian was no longer standing behind her but was down on one knee, holding an open box in his hand. She froze in place. Shock had overtaken her body and she couldn't speak or move.

"I love you Isabel Porter and I have for a very long time," declared Sebastian. "I don't ever want us to be apart again. Will you marry me?"

Chapter 27

Izzy stirred and stretched as she twisted herself awake. Opening her eyes, she felt someone staring at her. Gazing around the porch, her eyes landed on the culprit. There he was, sipping his coffee and staring at her.

"Why are you staring at me like that?" she asked feeling a little more self-conscious than normal. "After one look at me this morning you're regretting asking me to marry you, aren't you?" She laughed knowing what a hot mess she looked like in the mornings.

Sebastian walked over to the edge of the bed and sat down. "I was thinking about how I can't wait until I can wake up right next to you instead of you sleeping on my porch." He leaned down and kissed her on the forehead.

"I was thinking about that too last night," she said as she sat straight up in bed. "What do you think about us getting married in a few weeks?" Izzy's face scrunched up as if anticipating a negative reply.

Bash couldn't help but look shocked. Didn't most girls want months of excruciating planning and discussing and parties and drawing things out?

"Is that what you want?" he asked in amazement. "If you're asking me, I'd marry you today."

Izzy smiled and kissed him tenderly on the lips. "I don't want to waste any more time being apart. But do you think we can make it happen that fast?"

"Excuse me Ms. Porter," came the sing-songy southern drawl. "Do you know me at all? I would make anything happen for you."

Before he could finish his sentence, Izzy had popped out of bed and was already pacing. She was talking out loud but not necessarily to Bash. The to do list was being rattled off in rapid fire. Where would they get married? Would it be hard to find a venue with this short of notice? Who would they invite? Would it be a small quaint wedding, or did Sebastian have a list of people he wanted to come from Mobile? Would she be able to find a dress? Who would they ask to be in the wedding if anybody? Would they have a reception or just go without? Sebastian's brain was about to explode by the time he could grab hold of Izzy and sit her down on the side of the bed.

"Tell you what," he began in a very calming voice. "I will take care of the venue and you go look for a dress. Then we will come back tonight, regroup and start over again tomorrow."

"You're right," she replied. "One thing at a time. And maybe I'll recruit some help too."

Isabel ran home, showered and was down to greet Olivia when she arrived at the store. She could hardly contain her excitement but didn't want to burst out first thing with her happy news. She did everything she could think of to show off her ring. Laying books on the counter, she laid her hand on top of the stack and kept pointing to them hoping Olivia would just notice.

Finally, after many attempts, Izzy yelled out in excitement, "I'm engaged!"

Thankfully the store was empty so the screaming and jumping couldn't terrify unsuspecting customers. The two girls sounded like two clucking hens talking about the proposal, a desire for a quick wedding and details that needed to be handled. Olivia suggested a few shops where Izzy might find a dress on short notice and offered to call the florist. Isabel reiterated she wanted to keep everything simple. Everything about this wedding was to remain simple and as low stress as possible.

After a full day of shopping, Isabel found a beautiful, simple dress that would be perfect for their special day. Carrying a truck load of bags, she entered Sebastian's apartment exhausted. He ran over to relieve Izzy of her burden then guided her to the nearest seat.

"Are we sure I was the one who suggested a quick wedding?" asked Izzy laughing at herself. "Maybe I was just delirious and not fully awake this morning."

"Do you want me to make you feel better?" asked Bash with a sly grin on his face. "How would you feel if I told you I found a place for our wedding and reception?"

Izzy's eyes were wide in disbelief. "Tell me, tell me tell me," she exclaimed.

"We will be getting married at Double Oaks Farm and our reception will be in their barn." Sebastian smiled feeling very good about his efforts.

Tears of joy flowed down Isabel's cheeks as she realized her dreams were finally coming true.

Chapter 28

"Making a list and checking it twice," sang Isabel as she walked throughout the bookstore setting up decorations. "It's convenient I'm getting married the month of Christmas so I can sing that, and no one thinks I've lost my mind."

"I don't know if that's enough to guarantee your sanity," laughed Olivia as she watched her friend bouncing around in a frenzy. "Anyone who organizes a wedding in a couple of weeks then plans to get married in December can't be that sound of mind."

Izzy just laughed and continued decorating the store for the upcoming holiday. There was so much to be done between getting the store ready for the biggest selling season of the year and still crossing details off her wedding list. The bell on the door rang announcing a customer had arrived. Izzy turned to greet their visitor.

"Good morning ladies," stammered Asher. "I was wondering

if I could have a word with you Iz. I brought you a peace offering." He handed her a cup of hot coffee.

"I make no promises," she replied. "Why don't we take a walk outside."

Isabel walked to the back of the store with Asher following close behind. Going out the back door, she made her way to her favorite bench facing the bay. Asher sat down beside her, and they sat in silence, enjoying the view of the bay.

"Bash told me he proposed and ya'll are getting married," began Asher. "I want you to know how happy I am for you two." He paused to gather his thoughts. "You know Bash and I have been friends forever and he wants me to be his best man. But I can't do that unless I know that you and I are okay." He turned so he could look directly at Izzy.

She sat quietly, not immediately responding. Isabel wanted to take a moment and think through what she wanted to say. She turned to meet Asher's gaze.

"I was very angry with you Asher when I first discovered you were my stalker," replied Izzy. "But I've had some time to think about it. What I realized is what you meant for harm, turned out to be good."

Asher stared at her in amazement. What could his taunting have done that turned out for good?

"You see," she began. "I would have kept Sebastian at arm's length had it not been for the break-in and the continual gifts that frightened me. I would have never let him invade my life, my apartment like he did. But because I was afraid to be alone, I allowed him to stay. Bash living with me and caring for me caused my heart to gradually open up again. I'm not sure any of that would have happened if it hadn't been for you."

Asher didn't know how to respond. Was Izzy actually thanking him for what he had done?

"Don't get me wrong, Asher," leered Isabel. "What you did was wrong, but it turned out to be good."

"That's not the response I expected," replied Asher. "But I want to repeat to you again, how truly sorry I am for what I did. Just know it was only because I wanted to protect Bash. Do you think we can ever we be friends again?"

"I think I can manage that." Izzy stuck out her hand to shake in agreement.

"I'm sorry little lady," came the reply. "We hug in the south!" He grinned, put his arm around her shoulder and squeezed really tight.

****

Double Oak Farm was dressed to impress. Huge double oak trees lined both sides of the path. Underneath the trees sat white wooden chairs placed in rows. Strands of lights draped in the trees crisscrossed across the path and lit lanterns hung low in the branches. Buckets filled with baby's breath sat at the end of each row lining the path that led to the tulle-wrapped arbor with sparkling lights, where Izzy and Bash would recite their vows to each other.

The sun was a brilliant yellow red and had started its decent as the bridal party began their progression down the path. Izzy stood in awe realizing the perfect setting was happening on her perfect day.

Sebastian stared down the pathway trying to get a first glimpse of the woman who had stolen his heart. When she took her place at the top of the aisle, he had to catch his breath. Isabel Porter was a vision of simple elegance. Her dress had laced long sleeves due to the chill in the air. It was a light cream mixture of delicate lace and a swish of chiffon. It floated on air as she made her way down the aisle to meet the man who had won her heart. Twice. Isabel's dark brown eyes met Sebastian's and twinkled in delight. Her brunette hair had beads twisted throughout and was pulled to the side, gathered just near the bottom. As Izzy reached Bash's side, he looked down to see Ms. Dottie's pearls fastened tightly around her delicate neck. The final touch to complete the masterpiece. He brushed away a tear before taking Izzy's hands to begin his vows.

"It's hard to believe out of all the places you've traveled, somehow you ended up here—with me," started Sebastian. "It's truly a powerful thing and extremely humbling. There are many things I love about you and here are just a few:

I love your laugh, your smile and your caring nature.

I love the way you wrinkle up your nose when you think something is cute.

I love your dreams and passion. Those two things are what make you unique and wonderful.

I love it when your hair blows across your face when I'm looking into your eyes.

I love making you laugh when you are taking yourself too seriously.

I love that you lean on me and trust me with your care.

I love that you're loyal and faithful. Once you love, it's for always.

And I love that you want to make plans with me for our future. From this day forward I know I will have a partner and never walk alone."

Izzy brushed away a tear that escaped her eye. She hated to be emotional in front of people, but Sebastian's words went straight to her heart. Now it was Izzy's turn. It was hard to keep her hands from trembling as she unfolded her vows and began to read.

"There are a number of things I love about you, Bash," started Isabel, "And here are just a few:

I love that you are thoughtful and protective of me.

I love your ability to keep me grounded when I go off the rails.

I love that you wouldn't give up on us. Even though I'm stubborn and have made you swim a mote at times to reach me.

I love that you are strong, but you always make me feel

strong too. There's nothing we can't face if we stand together.

I love that you are so much more than I ever dreamed.

I know more than anything that I love you and I have to be with you. Everything else is just…details."

Sebastian didn't wait for his cue before he pulled Izzy into his arms and kissed his bride. Then he quickly escorted her down the pathway and when they reached the end, picked her up and twirled her around. Isabel squealed from delight and embarrassment. At least this time he didn't throw her over his shoulder.

The evening was spent hugging necks, receiving congrats from family and friends and dancing under the lights. As the music slowed, Bash drew Izzy into his arms. Whispering in her ear he said, "I remember every time I've made you blush, how you looked when you were soaked from head to toe by a water-fall, and the night when I held you close for the very first time. But tonight, when I saw this beautiful creature walking down the aisle towards little old me, that's an image I'll never forget. I love you Ms. Porter." Bash smiled and kissed his new wife.

"Excuse me?" she pulled away and smiled in proud delight. "You are now speaking to Mrs. Hadley."

A huge smile engulfed his face. "I love you dearly Mrs. Hadley."

Epilogue

Isabel sat and gazed up at the sky. It wouldn't be long before the sun was setting. The trickle of the fountain in the background along with the chirping of the crickets created its own sort of evening symphony. As she observed the beauty around her, she couldn't help but be thankful for the life she and Sebastian had created.

The marina had surpassed their wildest dreams over the past few years. Sebastian had worked out the kinks and made it one of the hottest Airbnb's on the southern coast. Bayfront Books had also excelled in its endeavors. Isabel continued to introduce new ideas along the way and the town responded causing the business to boom. They loved living life together in their small community.

Shortly after their wedding, they bought a nice piece of property outside of Fairhope and built a house. Izzy only asked for three things: a wrap-around front porch, a big kitchen, and a place she could relax on a back patio. Sebastian made all her dreams come true. The patio was designed to look just like Ms.

Dottie's garden area. Bash wouldn't let her see it until it was completely finished.

Izzy could hear the giggling before the two loves of her life came into full view. Periodically they would keep some of the horse rescues at their property to help out Bill and Georgia. Bash had taken their daughter out on a horseback ride and her heart just melted when she saw dad and daughter together.

Isabel walked out to meet them and took their daughter so Bash could unsaddle the horse and put her away for the night.

"Did you have fun, Dottie?" asked Isabel. "You sure look like you did because you're covered in dirt. Are you sure you left any out on the trail?"

Iz carried Dottie to the house, got her undressed and headed for the bathroom. Inside the master bath stood the beautiful claw foot tub from Ms. Dottie's house full of bubbles.

"Mommy tell me the story again," whined Dottie. "Where did I get my name?"

"Well, the lady who had this pretty bathtub at her house," explained Isabel. "Her name was Ms. Dottie, and she was some-one mommy and daddy loved very much."

"Oh yeah," smiled Dottie. "I forgot. I wish I could have met her."

"Me too darlin'," replied Izzy, a little teary eyed. "Me too."

Isabel had bathed and fed Dottie and put her to bed by the time Bash was finished brushing down the horse and putting things away. She was in the kitchen when he finally hauled himself inside.

"You really need to take a shower," smirked Isabel wrinkling up her nose.

"Are you offering to help?" came the broad grin that melted her heart.

"I've already bathed one of you tonight," she replied with a smile. "You're on your own."

Sebastian grabbed her around the waist and pulled her to him. "You said for better or worse Mrs. Hadley." Then he kissed her with all the love and passion he felt inside.

"Is that Ms. Dottie's iron skillet?" he asked finally letting her go.

"Why yes, it is," replied Isabel with a mischievous grin.

"So, what are we having for dinner then?" asked Bash out of curiosity.

Izzy couldn't hide the smile that spread across her face. "Chicken and Dumplings!"